To ~~[illegible]~~

Thanks so much for coming

Best wishes,

Carla Tomaso

UNHOLY ALLIANCES

•••

NEW WOMEN'S FICTION

UNHOLY ALLIANCES

◆ ◆ ◆

Edited by Louise Rafkin

Cleis Press
San Francisco ◆ Pittsburgh
1988

Published in the United States by Cleis Press, P.O. Box 8933, Pittsburgh, Pennsylvania 15221, and P.O. Box 14684, San Francisco, California 94114.

Printed in the United States.
Cover and text design: Louise Rafkin
Cover art: Pacha Wasiolek
Typesetting: Will Miner & his Wild Bats
First Edition.
10 9 8 7 6 5 4 3 2 1
ISBN: 0-939416-14-x cloth
ISBN: 0-939416-15-8 paper
Library of Congress Catalog Card Number: 88-70219

Cleis Press and the editor wish to thank Ellen Olson for her support of women writers.

"Blood Relations" by Dorothy Bryant first published in *Fiction Network*; reprinted by permission of the author. Copyright ©1987 by Dorothy Bryant. "What Would You Have Done?" by Marnie Mueller reprinted by permission of *Jewish Currents* and the author. Copyright ©1988 by *Jewish Currents*.

Haiku by Chiyo courtesy of the translator, David Ray. Copyright ©1980 by David Ray. Chiyo (Japan: 1703-1775) is considered one of most important woman haiku composers in the classical period. Emily Dickinson's poetry reprinted by permission of the publishers and trustees of Amherst College from *The Poems of Emily Dickinson*, ed. Thomas H. Johnson, Cambridge, MA: The Belknap Press of Harvard University Press. Copyright ©1951, 1955, 1979, 1983 by the President and Fellows of Harvard College. Quote from *The Bone People* reprinted by permission of Louisiana University Press. Copyright ©1983 by Keri Hulme.

I am grateful to all who helped me bring this book together:
Frédérique and Felice, for encouragement
Laura Lynn Brown, for editorial help
the January 2nd crew, for their diligence (and fine company!)
Sandy Hall, for her reading skill and sensitivity
Pacha Wasiolek, for her patience and generous talent
Sarah Ludden, for her support and perspective.
-L.R.

I'm Nobody! Who are you?
Are you—Nobody—Too?
Then there's a pair of us!

EMILY DICKINSON

◆ ◆ ◆

They were nothing more than people, by themselves. Even paired, any
pairing, they would have been nothing more than people by themselves.
But all together, they have become the heart and muscles and mind of
something perilous and new, something strange and growing and great.
Together, all together, they are the instruments of change.

KERI HULME
from The Bone People

◆ ◆ ◆

After a long winter, giving
each other nothing, we collide
with blossoms in our hands.

CHIYO

Translated by David Ray

♦ ♦ ♦

Contents:

$\blacklozenge$

Introduction

UNHOLY ALLIANCES. A troublesome couple of words?

My brother told me he'd never buy a book with this title. "Creepy," he said and then asked, after a moment, "But what does it mean?"

My explanation to him was long-winded and only somewhat successful. First of all, the stories in this collection aren't creepy. Some of them make me a bit uncomfortable, yes, perhaps a little uneasy. But there are those, too, that make me happy for life and for living. Some stories seem incredible—the kind you tell someone and they say, "No, really?" in a low voice. And stories that offer hope for understanding between people who are different, come from different places or cultures. *Unholy alliances*. Words that I have had tacked over my desk for the last couple of years. Words that suggest to me the way life is and the way life should be.

Yet there were others, besides my brother, who had a difficult time with this concept. I received letters from writers begging for explanation. And stories from those who assured me their work would fit the theme perfectly. Most often I didn't agree. And stories with timid cover letters, underscoring the writer's confusion. "I have no idea what you are looking for," one woman wrote honestly, "but here's something I just finished." A find!

For many the words "unholy alliances" translated directly into Bad Relationships: bad for her, bad for him, star-crossed, obsessive, tragic. I could have compiled another entire anthology under this theme, and perhaps someone should. (Given the success of the "Women Who Love Too Much" series, it could be a best-seller.) None of these stories of relationships-gone-bad struck me as that "unholy"—maybe it's because I was after something more unusual.

As in any collection, the bias of the editor is reflected in the book. I look for something in a story that excites me, writing that grabs a piece of life and illuminates it in such a way as to change the way I see the world. Stories where something happens and that something reflects the world as I know it, but goes on to suggest more. And I'm a pushover for a story that pulls at my heart. I like stories, too, that grapple with personal issues yet take into account the tough political and social realities of our time. After reading hundreds of manuscripts, the collection shaped itself around the theme, each piece adding to the whole.

Some of the stories in this anthology are by previously unpublished writers; other authors will be widely recognized for their novels or short stories. Some deserve their own collections and we will no doubt hear from them again. Bárbara Selfridge is one such deserving writer whose work bookends the collection. Her short-shorts are gems, distilling all of life into moments of connection. "I fell," says her narrator in "On Foot," and a busy Manhattan sidewalk is transformed into a place where strangers can play out their love for the world.

Joan Tollifson's story, "Watering the Plants," is a piece that makes my heart swell. Tollifson stacks up the separate lives of a slightly obsessive lesbian and a disabled male heterosexual in a way that transforms the mundane into the cosmic. In "Blood Relations," Dorothy Bryant sensitively explores the affinity between a gay man whose lover has AIDS and his widowed grandmother.

Other stories are not so kind: less alliance, more unholy. Winn

Gilmore's "Rev'ren Peach" tells the saga of a young black woman's sexual abuse at the hands of a town preacher. And Katharine Haake's lyrical study of a mother and daughter, in "All the Water in the World," lingers long after its wickedly eerie ending.

Still other pieces gather under the loose awning of outrageousness: the stark confederation of two strippers in Gita B. Carlstrom's "Hit the Beat," or the crazy-making post office transaction captured by Canyon Sam in "People Like This." And cross-cultural experiences often fall into the unholy realm, as shown quite literally in Marnie Mueller's glimpse into the marriage of a Jewish woman and her Nazi-descended husband.

There are also stories of families, somewhat of a traditional alliance. But each of these stories of familial ties contains some element of intrigue or insight that helps me file it with the rest of the "unholies." Deborah Rose O'Neal's story of half sisters in "Marguerite Marie" is a perfect example. And Patricia Roth Schwartz's "Sunspots" reads like a home-movie rendition of a woman estranged from her family.

There is a sense of urgency in the much of the work, a compulsion toward connection and intimacy. Characters reach across chasms to make contact, sometimes only a brief moment of understanding against a backdrop of personal confusion and the general stress of life in the eighties. And sometimes that moment is skewed, twisted, or missed altogether. But, nevertheless, there is the impulse towards the alliance. These are stories of allies and foes, strangers and strugglers. In many ways they are stories of the margin, of relationships just a bit off center. If life is a sidewalk, these are some of the cracks; you may avoid them, but they ultimately give shape to the path.

I'm most interested in these odd comings together. I'm hoping you (and my brother) are, too.

Oakland, California
February 1988

Bárbara Selfridge

◆

This Close to the End

I WAS THERE when the world ended. I'd been up all night,
waiting tables, half falling asleep, but now at dawn I was
clearheaded, sitting at a bus stop on Shattuck Avenue, and the
world was ending.

The end of the world came like the end of the night: the sun
starting as a molten sliver on the horizon, the sun moving up to
emit rays as thin as mechanical pencil leads. Dawn came three
times that morning, but each time the sun dropped back down,
and finally, overhead, they announced the end of the world.

First they joked: "Consider all strikes and labor disputes settled!"
Then they admitted: "As you may have noticed, the sun and earth
are out of sync. Dawn won't make it into day, the world won't into
tomorrow."

And there we were, in that funny place: the world at its end, but
as yet unended. Who knew what to do?

I ran into a man I knew, a man half-black, half-something else,
who plays pool somewhat professionally and buys coffee every
night from me. "The world is ending," he said. "How about it?"

He smiled pretty and added: "I've always wanted to."

I smiled back—"Okay"—because for months I'd wanted to, too, just not specifically with him. And sinking into his lips, running my tongue across his shoulder, I thought: *Just once before it all ends, I'll know sex without stress.*

Not so, however. My new friend jumped up, breaking off. Too many kisses, he said. Too much nuzzling. "Hey!" he said, and his name was Clarence. "I want to fuck before it ends, but that's not *all* I want to do!"

How funny! I thought, but I could see his point—hadn't I chosen an unmarried life for exactly those reasons?—and we dressed in perfect charity. The world was ending. Who knew what to do?

At Jack London Square, Clarence and I ran smack into a parade coming down Broadway. Not exactly a parade, just a lot of people getting married because who wants to end the world engaged? Black wedding parties, mostly, the mothers weeping in light orange gowns and everywhere striped waistcoats and gauzy sun hats.

Clarence walked away quickly—not wanting, in that crowd, to make an interracial scene. Not even then, at the end. I was hurt, but he was right. Because you think the world will die so different than it lives and it does but not really.

Julia Alvarez

♦

Daughter of Invention

S HE WANTED TO INVENT something, my mother. There was
a period after we arrived in this country, until five or so years
later, when my mother was inventing. They were never pressing,
global needs she was addressing with her pencil and pad. She
would have said that was for men to do, rockets and engines that
ran on gasoline and turned the wheels of the world. She was just
fussing with little house things, don't mind her.

She always invented at night, after settling her house down. On
his side of the bed my father would be conked out for an hour
already, his Spanish newspaper draped over his chest, his glasses,
propped up on his bedside table, looking out eerily at the darkened
room like a disembodied guard. But in her lighted corner, like some
devoted scholar burning the midnight oil, my mother was
inventing, sheets pulled to her lap, pillows propped up behind her,
her reading glasses riding the bridge of her nose like a
schoolmarm's. On her lap lay one of those innumerable pads of
paper my father always brought home from his office,
compliments of some pharmaceutical company, advertising

tranquilizers or antibiotics or skin cream; in her other hand, my
mother held a pencil that looked like a pen with a little cylinder of
lead inside. She would work on a sketch of something familiar, but
drawn at such close range so she could attach a special nozzle or
handier handle, the thing looked peculiar. Once, I mistook the
spiral of a corkscrew for a nautilus shell, but it could just as well
have been a galaxy forming.

It was the only time all day we'd catch her sitting down, for she
herself was living proof of the *perpetuum mobile* machine so many
inventors had sought over the ages. My sisters and I would seek her
out now when she seemed to have a moment to talk to us: We were
having trouble at school or we wanted her to persuade my father
to give us permission to go into the city or to a shopping mall or
a movie—in broad daylight! My mother would wave us out of her
room. "The problem with you girls. . ." I can tell you right now
what the problem always boiled down to: We wanted to become
Americans and my father—and my mother, at first—would have
none of it.

"You girls are going to drive me crazy!" She always threatened
if we kept nagging. "When I end up in Bellevue, you'll be safely
sorry!"

She spoke in English when she argued with us, even though, in
a matter of months, her daughters were the fluent ones. Her
English was much better than my father's, but it was still a
mishmash of mixed-up idioms and sayings that showed she was
"green behind the ears," as she called it.

If my sisters and I tried to get her to talk in Spanish, she'd snap,
"When in Rome, do unto the Romans. . ."

I had become the spokesman for my sisters, and I would stand
my ground in that bedroom. "We're not going to that school
anymore, Mami!"

"You have to." Her eyes would widen with worry. "In this
country, it is against the law not to go to school. You want us to get
thrown out?"

"You want us to get killed? Those kids were throwing stones today!"

"Sticks and stones don't break bones. . ." she chanted. I could tell, though, by the look on her face, it was as if one of those stones the kids had aimed at us had hit her. But she always pretended we were at fault. "What did you do to provoke them? It takes two to tangle, you know."

"Thanks, thanks a lot, Mom!" I'd storm out of that room and into mine. I never called her *Mom* except when I wanted her to feel how much she had failed us in this country. She was a good enough Mami, fussing and scolding and giving advice, but a terrible girlfriend parent, a real failure of a Mom.

Back she'd go to her pencil and pad, scribbling and tsking and tearing off paper, finally giving up, and taking up her *New York Times*. Some nights, though, she'd get a good idea, and she'd rush into my room, a flushed look on her face, her tablet of paper in her hand, a cursory knock on the door she'd just thrown open: "Do I have something to show you, Cukita!"

This was my time to myself, after I'd finished my homework, while my sisters were still downstairs watching TV in the basement. Hunched over my small desk, the overhead light turned off, my lamp shining poignantly on my paper, the rest of the room in warm, soft, uncreated darkness, I wrote my secret poems in my new language.

"You're going to ruin your eyes!" My mother would storm into my room, turning on the overly bright overhead light, scaring off whatever shy passion I had just begun coaxing out of a labyrinth of feelings with the blue thread of my writing.

"Oh Mami!" I'd cry out, my eyes blinking up at her. "I'm writing."

"Ay, Cukita." That was her communal pet name for whoever was in her favor. "Cukita, when I make a million, I'll buy you your very own typewriter." (I'd been nagging my mother for one just like the one father had bought her to do his order forms at home.) "Gravy on the turkey" was what she called it when someone was buttering her up. She'd butter and pour. "I'll hire you your very own typist."

Down she'd plop on my bed and hold out her pad to me. "Take a guess, Cukita?" I'd study her rough sketch a moment: soap sprayed from the nozzle head of a shower when you turned the knob a certain way? Coffee with creamer already mixed in? Time-released water capsules for your plants when you were away? A key chain with a timer that would go off when your parking meter was about to expire? (The ticking would help you find your keys easily if you mislaid them.) The famous one, famous only in hindsight, was the stick person dragging a square by a rope—a suitcase with wheels? "Oh, of course," we'd humor her. "What every household needs: a shower like a car wash, keys ticking like a bomb, luggage on a leash!" By now, as you can see, it'd become something of a family joke, our Thomas Edison Mami, our Benjamin Franklin Mom.

Her face would fall. "Come on now! Use your head." One more wrong guess, and she'd tell me, pressing with her pencil point the different highlights of this incredible new wonder. "Remember that time we took the car to Bear Mountain, and we re-ah-lized that we had forgotten to pack an opener with our pick-a-nick?" (We kept correcting her, but she insisted this is how it should be said.) "When we were ready to eat we didn't have any way to open the refreshments cans?" (This before fliptop lids, which she claimed had crossed her mind.) "You know what this is now?" A shake of my head. "Is a car bumper, but see this part is a removable can opener. So simple and yet so necessary, no?"

"Yeah, Mami. You should patent it." I'd shrug. She'd tear off the scratch paper and fold it, carefully, corner to corner, as if she were going to save it. But then, she'd toss it in the wastebasket on her way out of the room and give a little laugh like a disclaimer. "It's half of one or two dozen of another. . ."

I suppose none of her daughters was very encouraging. We

resented her spending time on those dumb inventions. Here, we were trying to fit in America among Americans; we needed help figuring out who we were, why these Irish kids whose grandparents were micks two generations ago, why they were calling us spics. Why had we come to the country in the first place? Important, crucial, final things, you see, and here was our own mother, who didn't have a second to help us puzzle any of this out, inventing gadgets to make life easier for American moms. Why, it seemed as if she were arming our own enemy against us!

One time, she did have a moment of triumph. Every night, she liked to read *The New York Times* in bed before turning off her light, to see what the Americans were up to. One night, she let out a yelp to wake up my father beside her, bolt upright, reaching for his glasses which, in his haste, he knocked across the room. "*Que pasa? Que pasa?*" What is wrong? There was terror in his voice, fear she'd seen in his eyes in the Dominican Republic before we left. We were being watched there; he was being followed; he and mother had often exchanged those looks. They could not talk, of course, though they must have whispered to each other in fear at night in the dark bed. Now in America, he was safe, a success even; his Centro Medico in Brooklyn was thronged with the sick and the homesick. But in dreams, he went back to those awful days and long nights, and my mother's screams confirmed his secret fear: we had not gotten away after all; they had come for us at last.

"Ay, Papi, I'm sorry. Go back to sleep, Cukito. It's nothing, nothing really." My mother held up the *Times* for him to squint at the small print, back page headline, one hand tapping all over the top of the bedside table for his glasses, the other rubbing his eyes to wakefulness.

"Remember, remember how I showed you that suitcase with little wheels so we would not have to carry those heavy bags when we traveled? Someone stole my idea and made a million!" She shook the paper in his face. She shook the paper in all our faces that night. "See! See! This man was no *bobo*! He didn't put all his pokers on a back burner. I kept telling you, one of these days my ship would pass me by in the night!" She wagged her finger at my sisters and my father and me, laughing all the while, one of those eerie laughs crazy people in movies laugh. We had congregated in her room to hear the good news she'd been yelling down the stairs, and now we eyed her and each other. I suppose we were all thinking the same thing: Wouldn't it be weird and sad if Mami did end up in Bellevue as she'd always threatened she might?

"*Ya, ya!* Enough!" She waved us out of her room at last. "There is no use trying to drink spilt milk, that's for sure."

It was the suitcase rollers that stopped my mother's hand; she had weather vaned a minor brainstorm. She would have to start taking herself seriously. That blocked the free play of her ingenuity. Besides, she had also begun working at my father's office, and at night, she was too tired and busy filling in columns with how much money they had made that day to be fooling with gadgets!

She did take up her pencil and pad one last time to help me out. In ninth grade, I was chosen by my English teacher, Sister Mary Joseph, to deliver the teacher's day address at the school assembly. Back in the Dominican Republic, I was a terrible student. No one could ever get me to sit down to a book. But in New York, I needed to settle somewhere, and the natives were unfriendly, the country inhospitable, so I took root in the language. By high school, the nuns were reading my stories and compositions out loud to my classmates as examples of imagination at work.

This time my imagination jammed. At first I didn't want and then I couldn't seem to write that speech. I suppose I should have thought of it as a "great honor," as my father called it. But I was mortified. I still had a pronounced lilt to my accent, and I did not like to speak in public, subjecting myself to my classmates' ridicule. Recently, they had begun to warm toward my sisters and me, and it took no great figuring to see that to deliver a eulogy for a convent full of crazy, old overweight nuns was no way to endear myself to the members of my class.

But I didn't know how to get out of it. Week after week, I'd sit down, hoping to polish off some quick, noncommittal little speech. I couldn't get anything down.

The weekend before our Monday morning assembly I went into a panic. My mother would just have to call in and say I was in the hospital, in a coma. I was in the Dominican Republic. Yeah, that was it! Recently, my father had been talking about going back home to live.

My mother tried to calm me down. "Just remember how Mister Lincoln couldn't think of anything to say at the Gettysburg, but then, Bang! 'Four score and once upon a time ago,'" she began reciting. Her verson of history was half invention and half truths and whatever else she needed to prove a point. "Something is going to come if you just relax. You'll see, like the Americans say, 'Necessity is the daughter of invention.' I'll help you."

All weekend, she kept coming into my room with help. "Please, Mami, just leave me alone, please," I pleaded with her. But I'd get rid of the goose only to have to contend with the gander. My father kept poking his head in the door just to see if I had "fulfilled my obligations," a phrase he'd used when we were a little younger, and he'd check to see whether we had gone to the bathroom before a car trip. Several times that weekend around the supper table, he'd recite his valedictorian speech from when he graduated from high school. He'd give me pointers on delivery, on the great orators and their tricks. (Humbleness and praise and falling silent with great emotion were his favorites.)

My mother sat across the table, the only one who seemed to be listening to him. My sisters and I were forgetting a lot of our Spanish, and my father's formal, florid diction was even harder to understand. But my mother smiled softly to herself, and turned the

Lazy Susan at the center of the table around and around as if it were the prime mover, the first gear of attention.

That Sunday evening, I was reading some poetry to get myself inspired: Whitman in an old book with an engraved cover my father had picked up in a thrift shop next to his office a few weeks back. "I celebrate myself and sing myself. . ." "He most honors my style who learns under it to destroy the teacher." The poet's words shocked and thrilled me. I had gotten used to the nuns, a literature of appropriate sentiments, poems with a message, expurgated texts. But here was a flesh and blood man, belching and laughing and sweating in poems. "Who touches this book touches a man."

That night, at last, I started to write, recklessly, three, five pages, looking up once only to see my father passing by the hall on tiptoe. When I was done, I read over my words, and my eyes filled. I finally sounded like myself in English!

As soon as I had finished that first draft, I called my mother to my room. She listened attentively, as she had to my father's speech, and in the end, her eyes were glistening too. Her face was soft and warm and proud. "That is a beautiful, beautiful speech, Cukita. I want for your father to hear it before he goes to sleep. Then I will type it for you, all right?"

Down the hall we went, the two of us, faces flushed with accomplishment. Into the master bedroom where my father was propped up on his pillows, still awake, reading the Dominican papers, already days old. He had become interested in his country's fate again. The dictatorship had been toppled. The interim government was going to hold the first free elections in thirty years. There was still some question in his mind whether or not we might want to move back. History was in the making, freedom and hope were in the air again! But my mother had gotten used to the life here. She did not want to go back to the old country where she was only a wife and a mother (and a failed one at that, since she had never had the required son). She did not come straight out and disagree with my father's plans. Instead, she fussed with him about reading the papers in bed, soiling those sheets with those poorly printed, foreign tabloids. *"The Times* is not that bad!" she'd claim if my father tried to humor her by saying they shared the same dirty habit.

The minute my father saw my mother and me, filing in, he put his paper down, and his face brightened as if at long last his wife had delivered a son, and that was the news we were bringing him. His teeth were already grinning from the glass of water next to his bedside lamp, so he lisped when he said, "Eh-speech, eh-speech!"

"It is so beautiful, Papi," my mother previewed him, turning the sound off on his TV. She sat down at the foot of the bed. I stood before both of them, blocking their view of the soldiers in helicopters landing amid silenced gun reports and explosions. A few weeks ago it had been the shores of the Dominican Republic. Now it was the jungles of Southeast Asia they were saving. My mother gave me the nod to begin reading.

I didn't need much encouragement. I put my nose to the fire, as my mother would have said, and read from start to finish without looking up. When I was done, I was a little embarrassed at my pride in my own words. I pretended to quibble with a phrase or two I was sure I'd be talked out of changing. I looked questioningly to my mother. Her face was radiant. She turned to share her pride with my father.

But the expression on his face shocked us both. His toothless mouth had collapsed into a dark zero. His eyes glared at me, then shifted to my mother, accusingly. In barely audible Spanish, as if secret microphones or informers were all about, he whispered, "You will permit her to read *that?"*

My mother's eyebrows shot up, her mouth fell open. In the old country, any whisper of a challenge to authority could bring the secret police in their black V.W.'s. But this was America. People could say what they thought. "What is wrong with her speech?" my mother questioned him.

"What ees wrrrong with her eh-speech?" My father wagged his head at her. His anger was always more frightening in his broken English. As if he had mutilated the language in his fury—and now there was nothing to stand between us and his raw, dumb anger. "What is wrong? I will tell you what is wrong. It shows no gratitude. It is boastful. 'I celebrate myself'? 'The best student learns to destroy the teacher'?" He mocked my plagiarized words. "That is insubordinate. It is improper. It is disrespecting of her teachers—" In his anger he had forgotten his fear of lurking spies: Each wrong he voiced was a decibel higher than the last outrage. Finally, he was yelling at me, "As your father, I forbid you to say that eh-speech!"

My mother leapt to her feet, a sign always that she was about to make a speech or deliver an ultimatum. She was a small woman, and she spoke all her pronouncements standing up, either for more protection or as a carry-over from her girlhood in convent schools where one asked for, and literally took, the floor in order to speak. She stood by my side, shoulder to shoulder; we looked down at my father. "That is no tone of voice, Eduardo—" she began.

By now, my father was truly furious. I suppose it was bad enough I was rebelling, but here was my mother joining forces with me. Soon he would be surrounded by a house full of independent American women. He too leapt from his bed, throwing off his covers. The Spanish newspapers flew across the room. He snatched my speech out of my hands, held it before my panicked eyes, a vengeful, mad look in his own, and then once, twice, three, four, countless times, he tore my prize into shreds.

"Are you crazy?" My mother lunged at him. "Have you gone mad? That is her speech for tomorrow you have torn up!"

"Have *you* gone mad?" He shook her away. "You were going to let her read that. . . that insult to her teachers?"

"Insult to her teachers!" My mother's face had crumpled up like a piece of paper. On it was written a love note to my father. Ever since they had come to this country, their life together was a constant war. "This is America, Papi, America!" she reminded him now. "You are not in a savage country any more!"

I was on my knees, weeping wildly, collecting all the little pieces of my speech, hoping that I could put it back together before the assembly tomorrow morning. But not even a sibyl could have made sense of all those scattered pieces of paper. All hope was lost. "He broke it, he broke it," I moaned as I picked up a handful of pieces.

Probably, if I had thought a moment about it, I would not have done what I did next. I would have realized my father had lost brothers and comrades to the dictator Trujillo. For the rest of his life, he would be haunted by blood in the streets and late night disappearances. Even after he had been in the states for years, he jumped if a black Volkswagen passed him on the street. He feared anyone in uniform: the meter maid giving out parking tickets, a museum guard approaching to tell him not to touch his favorite Goya at the Metropolitan.

I took a handful of the scraps I had gathered, stood up, and hurled them in his face. "Chapita!" I said in a low, ugly whisper. "You're just another Chapita!"

It took my father only a moment to register the hated nickname of our dictator, and he was after me. Down the halls we raced, but I was quicker than he and made it to my room just in time to lock the door as my father threw his weight against it. He called down curses on my head, ordered me on his authority as my father to open that door this very instant! He throttled that doorknob, but all to no avail. My mother's love of gadgets saved my hide that night. She had hired a locksmith to install good locks on all the bedroom doors after our house had been broken into while we were away the previous summer. In case burglars broke in again, and we were in the house, they'd have a second round of locks to contend with before they got to us.

"Eduardo," she tried to calm him down. "Don't you ruin my new locks."

He finally did calm down, his anger spent. I heard their footsteps retreating down the hall. I heard their door close, the clicking of their lock. Then, muffled voices, my mother's peaking in anger, in persuasion, my father's deep murmurs of explanation and of self-defense. At last, the house fell silent, before I heard, far off, the gun blasts and explosions, the serious, self-important voices of newscasters reporting their TV war.

A little while later, there was a quiet knock at my door, followed by a tentative attempt at the doorknob. "Cukita?" my mother whispered. "Open up, Cukita."

"Go away," I wailed, but we both knew I was glad she was there, and I needed only a moment's protest to save face before opening that door.

What we ended up doing that night was putting together a speech at the last moment. Two brief pages of stale compliments and the polite commonplaces on teachers, wrought by necessity without much invention by mother for daughter late into the night in the basement on the pad of paper and with the same pencil she had once used for her own inventions, for I was too upset to compose the speech myself. After it was drafted, she typed it up while I stood by, correcting her misnomers and mis-sayings.

She was so very proud of herself when I came home the next day with the success story of the assembly. The nuns had been flattered, the audience had stood up and given "our devoted teachers a standing ovation," what my mother had suggested they do at the end of my speech.

She clapped her hands together as I recreated the moment for her. "I stole that from your father's speech, remember? Remember how he put that in at the end?" She quoted him in Spanish, then translated for me into English.

That night, I watched him from the upstairs hall window where I'd retreated the minute I heard his car pull up in front of our house. Slowly, my father came up the driveway, a grim expression on his face as he grappled with a large, heavy cardboard box. At the front door, he set the package down carefully and patted all his pockets for his house keys—precisely why my mother had invented her ticking key chain. I heard the snapping open of the locks downstairs. Heard as he struggled to maneuver the box through the narrow doorway. Then, he called my name several times. But I would not answer him.

"My daughter, your father, he love you very much," he explained from the bottom of the stairs. "He just want to protect you." Finally, my mother came up and pleaded with me to go down and reconcile with him. "Your father did not mean to harm. You must pardon him. Always it is better to let bygones be forgotten, no?"

I guess she was right. Downstairs, I found him setting up a brand new electric typewriter on the kitchen table. It was even better than the one I'd been begging to get like my mother's. My father had outdone himself with all the extra features: a plastic carrying case with my initials, in decals, below the handle, a brace to lift the paper upright while I typed, an erase cartridge, an automatic margin tab, a plastic hood like a toaster cover to keep the dust away. Not even my mother, I think, could have invented such a machine!

But her inventing days were over just as mine were starting up with my schoolwide success. That's why I've always thought of that speech my mother wrote for me as her last invention rather than the suitcase rollers everyone else in the family remembers. It was as if she had passed on to me her pencil and pad and said, "Okay, Cukita, here's the buck. You give it a shot."

Joan Tollifson

◆

Watering the Plants

I CAN NEVER DECIDE what to do with my life. I pursue one interest and then another, never really finishing anything, except a painting from time to time. I'm an artist. I paint pictures. But I never sell them or exhibit them anywhere. I'm not famous. I do odd jobs, whatever I can get. I'm always worried about the future. I obsess about who to become and where to park the car. I can see myself ending up as a bag lady.

This morning, as I was driving Vivian to work, I glanced in the rear view mirror and saw a funeral procession pulling onto the highway behind us. I saw the black hearse and the long string of cars with headlights on. Vivian was watching me.

"You're so sexy," she said, sliding her hand along the inside of my thigh. She reached for my belt buckle. "We could stop at a motel, Annie."

I pushed her hand away, locking it in mine.

"Come on," she urged. "We'll both call in sick."

The car veered dangerously into the next lane.

"Stop it, Viv," I pleaded. "Don't do this to me during rush hour. It's dangerous."

Vivian's my newest girlfriend. We're having this very hot affair.

Stan leapt across his living room like a flying fish, landed lightly on one foot, and collapsed on the floor. He had wild black hair and dark intelligent eyes. He rolled and twisted into an upright position, and brought himself to his feet again, jerking forward once more into space, and catching himself on a doorjamb. He had attached the end of the long hose to the spigot on the kitchen sink. The task now was to drag the other end of the hose out onto the little porch that overlooked the city, where his collection of dry and dying plants sat in their huge pots. Once he got the hose out to the porch, he would return to the kitchen and turn on the water. Finally, maneuvering himself back out to the porch, he would aim the hose into each of the flower pots in turn.

We were parked now in front of the building where Vivian worked.

"You have such beautiful breasts," she told me.

"There's your boss," I warned. Mr. Carrington was crossing the street about half a block away, headed in our direction.

"Umm. I'd like to put them in my mouth and suck on them."

"Vivian, go on. You're going to make me late and drive me crazy. I'll see you Friday night."

Our hands played together on the seat between us. Mr. Carrington disappeared into the building. Vivian kissed me on the neck, and slid out of the car. All I could think of was sex.

Stan had the hose in both hands now and was falling through the air, plummeting toward the porch. He ricocheted off a chair, bounced twice on one foot like a ballet dancer, and crash landed gracefully against the wall, the hose still clutched between his strong hands. His dark eyes gleaming. He smiled triumphantly and lunged forward, pulling the hose onto the porch.

I was still thinking of sex when a horn blared and a taxicab screeched to a stop beside me at a red light.

"Fucking bitch!" the driver yelled fiercely at me. "It's idiots like you that make the roads unsafe!"

"Cram it, buddy!" I yelled back. "I don't know what the hell you're talking about!"

"Goddamn idiot! You swerved right in front of me! You weren't paying attention at all! Could have killed us both, lady! They should keep people like you off the roads!"

"Hah!" I yelled back. "You were probably going too damned fast and now you're trying to blame it on me! It's a wonder there's anyone left alive in this city with all you fucking cab drivers speeding around the way you do!"

We were both red in the face. The light turned green. We were still glaring at each other. Suddenly he broke into a beautiful smile. "Hey. . . have a nice day!" he said.

"You, too!" I smiled back.

We drove off. I was no longer thinking about sex.

On his second attempt, Stan had gotten the nozzle of the hose lodged securely in one of the larger pots. He was dancing back toward the kitchen now, bouncing and falling, catching himself, twirling toward the water tap. He reached for it, balancing himself on the sink, leaning forward precariously, and turned on the water. He executed a daring 180-degree turn, veered out into the living room, crashed to the floor, and crawled back out to the porch. Below him, the city was busy with morning traffic. Seagulls swept through the air above him. He paused for a moment to drink in these impressions, and then lunged for the hose, capturing it in his hands.

I got a parking place right in front of the office where I work! Burbank, Antonelli and Woo—Attorneys at Law. I'm their secretary. The office is smoky when I walk in, and reeks of overflowing ashtrays. Harley Burbank has been there all night, working on a case. He is hunched over his desk, his face ashen gray, his eyes red, his hair in complete disorder, a cigarette hanging from his lips. I flick on the lights in the hall, feed the tropical fish, turn on my computer and the lights in my office, and pour myself a cup of coffee. I sit down. My desk is covered with 8 x 10 glossy photographs of a dead man lying nude on a table at the morgue. The man's arms are tattooed with swastikas. I see multiple bullet holes in the flesh, some marked with red arrows.

Stan was watering the plants now. Aiming the hose carefully into the pots, losing control occasionally, the water shooting out in different directions, sometimes over the edge of the balcony, or into the glass doors. Stan was pretty wet himself. He was laughing. His eyes were fierce black beacons. Everything was wet!

I had started thinking about sex again. I was typing up divorce papers. Then, without a moment's notice, I found myself pondering my future. I saw that bag lady pushing her shopping cart into my mind again. What was I doing with my life? Maybe I should settle down and get serious about something, or someone. Like Vivian, or my painting. Maybe I could be a Great Artist. Or maybe I should do something more financially sound, like go to law school. If I wasn't careful, I'd be on my deathbed trying to decide what to be when I grew up, having lived nothing but a life of part-time love affairs and temporary jobs. Would Vivian and I stay together? Should I go to law school? If not that, then what? Which freeway should I take tonight? Would Vivian and I have sex on Friday when I saw her again? Should I refuse to have sex, so we could get some sleep? I needed some sleep. Where should I have lunch? Would I ever be able to find such a perfect parking place again?

Stan lay on his side, laughing, clutching the hose in both hands. Water shooting out, the plants drinking it up. Stan rolling from side to side. The hose shooting water over the edge of the balcony, the pedestrians down below looking up and cursing. Finally, making a sound like a wild bull, Stan flipped himself over one last time. Water crashed into the glass doors, narrowly missing the living room. He drew himself up onto his knees and carefully maneuvered the nozzle of the hose into one of the larger pots. Then he pulled himself up and dove back into the apartment.

Maybe I *should* go to law school. I have to be *something*, after all! But I'd hate law school. It would ruin my mind. I'd go crazy. I *am* going crazy thinking and typing all these papers day after day. I wish I were doing something meaningful, or enjoyable. Something that paid me enough so I wasn't always in debt. I wondered what Vivian was doing. Selling computers, probably. The phone rang.
"Burbank, Antonelli & Woo—"
"Hi." It was Vivian. "Guess what? I just successfully impersonated a computer salesman again and sold an entire line of new computers to one of the biggest stores in town at a fantastic profit *and* I may get a big promotion!"

"What are they going to pay you now?"

"I won't settle for anything less than seventy-five grand a year this time."

Vivian was making money like crazy, *and* being a successful photographer (she had two shows last year), *and* was thinking of having a baby. Soon she would be succeeding brilliantly at business, art and motherhood simultaneously. I, meanwhile, was in debt, un-exhibited, and barely able to take care of my cat.

"Of course," Vivian was saying, "I may have to work more."

"Work more!? You're already working fifty hours a week at least! Not to mention the time you spend in the darkroom! I'll never see you! You'll be miserable! I thought you were going to have a baby?"

"Well, I might not get the promotion. Anyway, I was thinking we could have dinner tonight. Go out to some really nice restaurant for a treat. What do you say?"

"I can't. I'm having dinner with Stan. I told you that."

"Who?"

"My friend Stan. The writer. You know, the guy in the wheelchair who can't talk very well. Remember? He called one night and totally freaked you out."

"He didn't totally freak me out."

"He did. I could tell." The phone rang again. "Gotta go, Viv. Don't kiss." I pushed the button. "Burbank, Antonelli and Woo—"

Stan lunged into the bedroom, bouncing off the walls, and fell against the dresser. He took out a dry pair of pants and tossed them onto the bed. He danced over to the closet, bouncing on one foot, catching himself on the doorjamb. He picked out a fresh shirt. He tossed it onto the bed. Then he hurled himself onto the bed after them, and began wrestling himself out of the wet clothes he was wearing, and into the dry ones. It took him about twenty-five minutes. Then he had to put on shoes and socks, and brush his hair. That took another fifteen minutes. Finally he was dressed and ready to go. He spun out into the living room, crashing against his desk, grabbing onto a chair for support, bouncing across the floor, and landed neatly in his electric wheelchair.

I move like abstract art, he thought to himself. Zipping over to his desk, he turned on his computer. Losing my balance and regaining it again, I give myself to the void, he wrote, his long, untameable fingers flying over the keys like drunken hummingbirds.

Finally he gathered a stack of papers in his arms, and whizzed out of the apartment, down the corridor, aiming his whole being at the little black elevator button, hitting it on the first shot. He waited, then glided onto the elevator, rode down and whizzed out the front door of the building into the bright sunlight. He wasn't prepared for the sudden wind. It picked up his papers and blew them into the street. He groaned. A man coming down the sidewalk saw what happened and broke into a run, quickly rescuing all the papers. Gathering them together, the man approached Stan nervously, as if he were approaching an alien from another planet.

"Here. . . Ah, where do you want these?" There was moisture on the man's brow.

Stan reached for his papers and the man recoiled slightly.

"Here. . . I'll just put them in your pack here for you," the man said quickly, spotting the backpack slung over the back of Stan's chair, and moving toward it.

Stan opened his mouth to protest but nothing came out except a strange sound. He pressed his fingers into the sides of his neck, which helped him speak, and tried again. He made a choking sound this time. The man was desperately stuffing the papers into the pack behind Stan. "Nnno," Stan said finally. "I wwwaaant to hhhaaa—ve ttthem hhhere."

The man looked terrified. "I put them all in your pack for you," he said paternally, as if talking to a very young child, and patted Stan on the head. "They'll be safe there. You have a good day now," and he hurried off down the street.

I can't believe that my purpose in life is to answer phones and type letters for Burbank, Antonelli and Woo. Of course, I paint. But is my painting truly good? I worry about this kind of thing. I also study Kung Fu. Maybe after I get my black belt I can teach Kung Fu, open my own school. No, I'm probably too old. I'll be forty before I get my black belt. Besides, I'm too clumsy. Law school would be safer. The noon whistle goes off like an air raid. Lunch time. I start thinking about the man in the picture with the bullet holes. I worry about the future.

Stan whizzed along, the wind hitting his face, the green trees speeding past him. Children stared, their mouths hanging open in horror. One little girl screamed at the sight of him and covered her eyes. He sped on. It was high noon. He was going shopping.

I spent the afternoon transcribing testimony from a seventeen-year-old heroin addict Harley was defending who had stabbed a seventy-year-old woman in the back for ten dollars. There was no possible good outcome. The kid's whole life had been miserable. The lady was dead. The autopsy photos were on my desk. I saw too many dead bodies on this job. I thought about my painting. I thought about my future. I thought about death. I thought about law school.

Stan had cooked fettucini with clam sauce. I arrived slightly late. I'd been in a traffic jam, worrying about my possible career as a lawyer. Stan's eyes were dark and shining, and he hurled himself gracefully through the space of the small apartment, crashing into walls, bouncing and twirling, as he ushered me in. I smiled, hugging him. His apartment was warm and cozy, his poems were tacked up on the walls, interspersed with some pencil sketches I had done and a poster that said "Stop the Bombing of El Salvador."

"Whaaaat did yoooou dooooo tooodaaay?" he asked. I strained, concentrating on every sound, struggling to understand.

"Two murders, a divorce, and a rape. I typed. I filed. I answered the phone. I hate my job," I replied.

Stan's hair was dark, his body slender, his hands thin and strong. He moved like some amazing dancer. His eyes were full of ironies and dark corners. I tried to imagine what it would be like having sex with him. Unlike anything else probably. Him flopping around like a fish out of control. Of course, he was probably a great lover. He had an incredible mind.

But it would be hard work having to concentrate so hard all the time to understand him. Spending half an hour listening to a few sentences that anyone else would say in a few minutes. And having to put up with the ways people treated him on the streets.

"What is it like having sex with you?" I asked boldly.

His eyes lit up. He laughed. "Mmmyyy lllaaaast girrrrl——ffrrrrrrriend.....uuuummmmmm.......I bbbrrrrrroke hhheerrr rrrrribs acccccidennntally......" Stan choked out nothing but air. He pressed the side of his neck and tried again. "uuummmmmmmm........wwwwiiith mmmmy eeelllllbow Ummmmmmm. In beddd. Ummmmmm."

"Umm."

"Whhhaat is ittt lllllike hhhaaaaving ssssex wwwwwwith yyy——yyy——yyyyy———ooooooooo?"

"With me?"

"Ummmm...." He nodded.

"Well, I don't know..."

"Dooooo yyoooooou bbbrrrrrrreaaaak Vi—Viiiiiivian's rrriibs?"

"Not yet."

He smiled. "Aaaaaffter yooooou get yoooourr bbbbbllllllack bbbbbeeellllt!"

"Yeah, right. So tell me what you did today," I asked him, "other than cook dinner?"

"Toooo-dddaaaay," he said, "I waaaat—" he pressed the side of his neck. Nothing came out but sounds. And then, "I waaaatered mmmmy plllllaaaaaaaaa——nntsss."

"What?" I asked.

"Toooday I waaatered mmy pllaants," he repeated.

"Oh, you watered your plants! Great."

"Ummm," he agreed with a trace of irony. "Grrreaaat. Theeeey were thirrrrrrrsty." He smiled. He went on to tell me about his papers scattering in the wind, and the man who rescued them. He told the story in great detail. It took a long time. I had to concentrate very hard to understand.

"I llllooove ttto ttellll lllllooooong stooo——rrrrries," he smiled, his eyes full of mischief and light.

"I've been obsessing about my future," I told him. "Law school. Painting. What to do."

"Yyyyyoooouuu'rre aan aarrrrrrrtt——ist, Aaaaannnie!" he said emphatically.

"But maybe I'm not that good at it, Stan."

"Dooooooooo yoooou e——en———jjjjjoooooooy it?"

"Do I enjoy it?"

He nodded vigorously.

I didn't usually think about things from that angle. I smiled. "You know, when I was a little kid, my mother used to give me a pail of water and a paint brush, and I'd paint the sidewalk with water. I loved it. It didn't matter to me at all that my work would evaporate and disappear. I loved the feel of every stroke, and the way the wet cement looked. I could paint the sidewalk like that for hours and be totally happy."

"Yyyyooooooouu wwwere a ggrrrrrrreeeeat pppppaaaaainnnter

ttthen." He grinned and his face grew serious. He pressed on the side of his neck. "A trrrrue mmaaaaaaster," he continued. "Yyyyou uuunder——sssssstooooood ttthe ssssssssseeeeeecret of ttiiiiiiiiime."

A painting started to take shape in the tips of my fingers. I felt it coming. It was a painting of water. Actually it was a picture of the whole universe and how I found the courage to swim.

Stan was laughing. He understood the secret of water.

Winn Gilmore

◆

Rev'ren Peach

W HEN I FIRST start showin, evrybody wonder who baby
it was. "It *mine*," I say. The ole mens laugh like they
knowed a secret, thowin back they kinky heads an showin they
tobacco-browned teeth.

An ole *womens*? They biddies. They frown up they faces like I
hadn took no bath in two weeks.

"Lawd, Lawd," they say. "In *my* day. . ." an they start cluckin they
tongues like fuckin was somethin today's young folks just thunk up.
An I knows for a *fac* that folks been doin it for years. . . centuries,
probly. My momma an her boyfriens does it all the time. An her
friens, the ole biddies what go to Church on Sunday an call me
"hoe" on Monday, they does it, too. An *I* don even *like* it.

Never will forget the time I was sneakin dandeline greens outta
Miz Johnson yard, an Rev'ren Peach come by to see her. When
Miz Johnson get to the door, she didn know who was there. (She
bout blind as a bat, anyhow.) Her face was all scrunch up like a

rotten prune some chile had done chewed up an spit out. *Then* she seed it was the Rev'ren.

(He ain *really* no preacher, though. Ain got no Church or *nothin*. Now his pappy, *he* was a preacher. Had a purty big Church, too, I heah tell. Then he die an his son, "Rev'ren" Peach, took ovah the Church an burnt it to. the groun. Said the Lawd tole him to, cause Sinnin had done been goin on in it. "Iffen thy left han offend thee, cut it off!" he be preachin an so on.

I reckon he took that to mean, "Iffen the folks in thy Church offend thee, burn em up!" Yep. He killed two folks in that fire, an I *know* the Bible don say to do that! Even if thy left han *an* thy right offend thee.

So, the white folks, they put him in the nut house for a lil while, but then they let him back out. Then he start standin on the street corner for a month a Sundays, yellin how God come to him in the nut house an tole him to get outta there an preach His Wuhd to Sinnahs. He preached, awright. Preach so hard the white policemens say they was gonna put him in jail for upsettin the peace. Dat kinda funny, though, I thinks. He kill two peoples an they puts him in the nut house just long enuff for ya to sneeze twice. He stan outdoors preachin an they wanna bust his head open an put him in jail. But "Dat's the law," they say.

Churchfolks an Sinnahs, too, they all stan roun laughin at Rev'ren Peach. An sometime they brung they chirrens. The chirrens like *him* better they like goin to the circus on Colored Folks Day.

So, young Rev'ren Blackman, he took Rev'ren Peach in an fed him so's he wouldn haveta get locked up in the jailhouse. The Churchfolks got *real* mad then, cause they didn like no parts of Rev'ren Blackman. Said he was a devil, a evil man tryin to bring Sin while he was all dressed up like a man of the Wuhd.

Said he could take all them newfangle idees rat back where he come from.

So, then they start sayin how Rev'ren Peach *had* done seed the Miracle of the Lawd in the nut house. They yank him outta Rev'ren Blackman house fast as lightnin. Start givin him bout as much *respec* as lightnin, too. Still, I knowed he weren no real preacher, this Rev'ren Peach.)

Now, where was I? Oh, yeah. When Miz Johnson seed who was at her front door, all the wrankles plumb drop outta her ole face. She lit up like a junebug in a Mason jar. This hoe-callin woman, she said, "Rev'ren Peach, how nice to see you on this day the Lawd have done give us." Said it so sweet, the wuhds floated like the stank of overripe tomatoes to where I was hidin in her yard, holdin the dandelines close to my ches. Thought I was gonna puke.

"Aftanoon, Sis Johnson," the shrivel-up, so-called preacher said. The screen door, then the front door, banged behin em when they went inside.

It was hottern Hades, one a them Missippi days where folks jes sits roun on they front porch not even botherin to fan theyselves cause it jes make they awready sweaty clothes stick to em more. Like dogs layin up under a shade tree, paws stretched all out an tongues lollin while flies jes a-buzz roun em. It was that kinda day. So, natchelly, I couldn figure out how come Miz Johnson shet her big front door after the Rev'ren go in. It was open *befo*.

So, of course, I tippy-toes up to a window an looks in, an whacha thinks I sees? Look like Miz Johnson was a-prayin, cause she be on her knees, an her head be noddin up an down, up an down, tween Rev'ren Peach legs. I thought sholy she was a-prayin for some Sin she had done, cause Rev'ren Peach had his hands on top her head, an he was saing, "Yes, Lawd, oooohhhh yes! *Jeeezus!!*" He shout so loud I almos scream an give way that I was watchin. Ida been in hot water for sho then! "Lawd, fahgive this head Sinnah woman. Oooohhh, yes!"

An I thought the Holy Ghose musta got in him, cause Rev'ren Peach body start twitchin an pumpin like a stuck pig. Like soma them Sistahs' bodies do when they be shoutin in Church on Sundays. "This heah is my body! Yes, Lawd, it is! Take: Eat. Do this, ohh *pleez* do this in memry of me!! Ohh, Jesus. Take, ummmm, this heah woman Sins an wash her white as snow!!"

I stared, amazed-like. Miz Johnson made a gaggin soun, an then she pull back. Then I seed what was *really* goin on. Rev'ren Peach, he squinch up his face an grab hisself where Miz Johnson mouth had been. His thing was all fat an swole up. It look like it were alive. Both me an Miz Johnson couldn take our eyes offa it, an Rev'ren Peach he pump hisself like he primin a well-pump, hard an fas. He look all crazy-like at Miz Johnson kneelin a little ways off from him, kneelin like she was waitin for somethin.

Rev'ren Peach pant like he jes preach a sermon to rock the gates of heaven *an* hell. "I baptizes you, ohhh, in the name a the Fathah," an some thick, snotty-lookin stuff shot outta his thing, "an the Son, an the Holy Ghose!!"

Miz Johnson face was all covered up with that snot-stuff. She smile, happy, like she jes been blessed.

"Yes, Lawd! Yes!!" she yell. They moans mixed, remindin me of revival folks screamin in the dead of a empty, sticky-hot night. Beggin Jesus to come an take em where they won't have no more cares-of-this-evil-worl. Rev'ren Peach fell down on his knees an start preachin, his thing all shrivel up now like a dried-out an sour piece a sausage. Miz Johnson, she lick her lips.

(I nevah was too hot on Church, but my momma made me go evry Sunday. She still be stankin from gin an fuckin on Sadday night when we trudge up the hill to the lil Church to sing "Amazin grace, how sweet the soun that save a retch like me!" In fac, it were the Sunday aftah I had done spied thu Miz Johnson window an seed her with Rev'ren Peach, when it happened.)

I weren saved, so momma made me sit on the mournin bench an beg Jesus to come in my soul. The Brothahs an the Preacher swayed an tremble in a circle roun me. They put they sweaty hans on my head while I kneel down. My head spose to be bowed down, but I look up jes far enough to see somethin growin in the Brothahs' pants. The whole Church was a-rockin back an forth, Saints clappin they hans an singin or moanin in they thoats. I reckon they couldn see the Preacher an Brothahs movin in real close to me, they britches fronts brushin up agins my face an hair. The moanin grew to a rumble, like that terrble soun what come befo a thunderclap.

I was scared. I shook an cried. The Preacher was sayin, "Come to Jesus, Sinnah gal!" I was scared an . . . confused. Did comin to Jesus have to do with what they was tryin to stick in my face? Like Miz Johnson an Rev'ren Peach? Was I a Sinnah cause I hadn let none of em do it to me? If I let em do it, would I be save? I start spinnin, goin in circles like a chicken with it head chopped off. Sistahs start shoutin an the singin got loud. *Real* loud. Way too loud. I couldn breathe no mo. Brothahs stuck-out pants comin in on me. Rev'ren Peach an Miz Johnson. That snot-lookin stuff all over her face an her lookin like . . . like . . . like she was happy, cause the Rev'ren had done jes save her. That awful moanin rumble finally give way to a thunderclap what almos split me in two. I blanked out.

"Chile, you'se gotta start thinkin bout yow *filthy* soul!" Me an momma was walkin home aftah my faintin spell. "You'se gotta let the Good Lawd in ya befo somethin *else* gits in ya." Momma look down at me, smilin nasty, like gin an fuckin. "Yep, you twelf now. You developin." I start feelin shame an nasty, like I done somethin bad. I didn know how come. I hunched up my shoulders, tryin to cover up the knots-turnin-into-mounds on my ches. I felt like a Sinnah. "You cain go roun Sinnin, jes a-temptin mens. Iffen you does, you gonna git jes what comin to you!"

Brothah Petah walk up longside momma, an she stop talkin at me. She start a-switchin her behin, makin her too-too tight skirt stick like honey to her big thighs an butt. She look like she had done been poured inta that skirt.

Brothah Petah grin like he jes seed the Lawd's body. "Ahem, Sistah," he clear his thoat an say. "So nice to see you on this heah day they Lawd have done give us." His smile jes bout split his face in two. I thought maybe the top a his head was gonna fall off an roll rat down the dirt road. At leas *then* he wouldn look at momma like he wanna chew her up an spit her out. "I wondah iffen you like ta come ovah to my house an dis-cuss the Wuhd a the Lawd. Goin to Church ain enough to save a soul, you know."

An momma she look down at his britches, smilin. Seem like all the birds stop singin. Seem like they weren a soun in the whole wide worl. I was holdin my breath, waitin for momma to say, "Thank ya kindly, Brothah Petah, but I gots ta go fix some suppah for this heah gal a mine." I pulled on her too-tight skirt.

She push me away an say, "Why sholy, Bro Petah. You mighty rat. You gone home, chile," she say to me. "I be home aftah I studies some *Scrip*shuh with the Brothah." An the birds, they start screechin like fingahnails on a chalkboard. I be feelin real dizzy agin. I wanna say, "No, momma! He gone do what Rev'ren Peach done to Miz Johnson. I gotta *talk* to you, momma! I needs to *know* somethin." But I kep my mouth shet, cause I was scared I was gonna puke. An anyhow, they had done awready start walkin toward Brothah Petah house. I headed for home.

When I got home, he was sittin on us front porch.

"Aftahnoon, honeychile." He start rubbin tween his legs.

"Aftahnoon, Rev'ren Peach." I look down at my shoes an hunch ovah my shoulders, cause I didn wanna temp him, like momma she say I might do to mens.

"Mighty good suhvice, huh?" I knowed he was a-starin at my ches when he started up a crazy laugh. I was scared. Momma, where you is?!

"Where yo momma, gal?"

I heard the rollin thunder agin, an dat crack what started rat befo I blacked out in Church, it jes split rat down the middle a me. Split wide open like a earthquake. An my *soul*. I felt it slippin way down tween the crack that was me. Look like I was gonna have ta let they Jesus inside a me aftah all. Look like I didn have no sayso.

"She gone home with Brothah Petah to study the Lawd's Wuhd," I say real sof. Felt tears wellin up behin my eyeballs. My legs lock theyselves togedder. Felt like I was dead, cause I was gonna have ta give up to they Jesus.

Rev'ren Peach thowed back his head an laugh, like God had done give him all he axe for. He thowed open his legs an I seed somethin pokin agins his britches. I knowed then I weren mine no mo. I was at they God's mercy.

"Well, lil Sistah," he said, smilin, "yo momma gone be studyin a *long* ole time, cause Bro Petah got a *lot* to teach her. Not as much as I gots to teach *you*, unnerstan." He walk to the edge a the porch. I was standin on a step. He took his thing outta his pants, an it stared me rat in the face. "Come on inside, lil Sistah. Yo momma be *real* mad she heah you thow me outta huh house while Ima jes tryin to save yo Sinnin soul, now won she?" He smile real crazy agin, an I wish he was back in the nut house. Back where the white folks law keep him from hurtin me. We went inside.

Momma she come home real late that night. She stumble inta my room, smellin like gin an that stuff Rev'ren Peach had done shot up inside a me. I seen her like I hadn nevah seen her befo. It was like covers had been snatched offa a dead an stankin body. I wanned to puke an cry an kill, all at the same time.

"How my baby gal?" she say. She try to smile, but she look all sad empty. Her smile look like she almos dead, like she wanna be dead. I wanned to be dead, too. I puked up all the rotten I had done an seed. Confessed bout Rev'ren Peach an Miz Johnson, bout Rev'ren Peach an what he done to me that day whiles she was out "studyin the Wuhd," bout his stabbin his thing up me an makin me bleed an hurt. Bout his preachin whiles he done it, sayin this what a *real* Christen woman spose to do, cause God say a woman lowern a man. A man spose to rule a woman. It God plan. An I reckon they God mean it, cause I had done read it in the Bible.

I showed her the bloody, stankin sheet.

She beat me till I couldn cry no mo. Till I pass out.

She beat me evry day aftah she come home drunk. Stankin like gin an mens. Beat me Sadday night, sayin I musta let some Sinnah boy fuck me. I musta temp him to come an do it. I was a Sinnah for sho. A devil. A evil gal-woman.

"Ain nothin for to do but *beat* God inta you! You a hoe, a no-good tramp tryin to brang down good Christens names. A fine man like Rev'ren Peach! A God-fearin woman like Sis Johnson! As the Good Lawd my witness, hoe, Ima kill you!!" She look like she was sad, mad, glad, crazy, all in one. I didn feel nothin, cep maybe I *was* a hoe, like maybe cause I had done refuse the Lawd I *shoulda* been all hurt up an abused by the Rev'ren, an like I was a Sinnah cause I didn like it like Miz Johnson did, like I reckon momma did. Like I shoulda been beat up by momma whiles she cry an scream an yell. She look like what Joseph musta look like when Mary say she ain fuck nobody to get pregnan. Mad as Hades. Wantin to heah anythin but the truth. So Mary lied. Said it were hern an the Holy Ghose baby.

Momma had all the Saints in Church pray for me that next Sunday. Said the Devil was in me. I sat up on the mournin bench, shakin an achin. I was a-hurtin from all the beatins, from bein stupid, from momma not believin me. I cried.

When I went down on my knees in front a all them men's hard things strugglin to git outta they pants, while they prayed ovah me, somethin happened deep inside. In a place what I thought had been killed las Sunday when I was split open by Rev'ren Peach an momma's belt. Rev'ren Peach, he was standin in front a me too, cause he was the gues preacher that day.

His britches was stickin out too. Like all the Brothahs who was standin roun me with they hans on my head. Somethin was happenin deep inside a me, an I start laughin. I wanned to take they things in my mouth an jes bite em off. An then I start screamin an cryin. Miz Johnson. Momma. Me. How many mo womens in the Church? I screamed outta pain an fear. I had done missed my monthly.

Rev'ren Peach look out at the Churchfolks an he say, "See, Sinnahs an Saints! The Lawd *do* wuhk in mys*eee*rious ways!!"

He musta thought I had done been took by the Holy Ghose. I look at his face. He was grinnin from ear to ear. He had done brung me to the Lawd. He had done been in the nut house an got out. He had done gone thu the fire, like them Christens in the Ole Testamen. He was a hero. He was a God. God was in his pants. The Lawd had took me.

So, when I first start showin, evrybody axe me who baby it was. "IT MINE!" I scream at em. The ole mens laugh like they knowed a secret. They thought they did. They thought God was in they pants, too. Ole womens screwed up they faces like I hadn had no bath in two weeks. "Lawd, Lawd! In *my* day!"

An I kep on gittin biggah. Till I knowed I was gonna pop wide open an spill the poison outta me. Momma still beat me. Tole me I was a hoe to let some Sinnah boy fuck me. She start gittin drunkern she useta. I wanned to make her mad. Her, Rev'ren Peach, an all the Saints! So I start sayin, when they axe me who baby it was, I say,

"It mine! Mine an the Holy Ghose! Jes like the Virgin Mary! That what she say an yall believes it! Well, that jes exackly what happen to me!" An I laugh like I ain nevah gone stop, it so funny to me. I tell em that in Church, on the street, evrywhere I goed. They start sayin somethin wrong with me in the head, but I didn *even* much care. Cause I knowed bout them an they God.

One day I was walkin home, slow as a sow stuck in her own mess. Churchfolk was lookin at me like I was crazy or evil. "Uh-huhn," they say shakin they heads. "That there gal ain right. Ain no God in *huh!*"

Now, what they wanna say that for? That jes make me maddern I awready were. I propped my han on my back an yell, "The 'Holy Ghose' have done entered inta me jes like it have yall!! Cause I sees Rev'ren Peach an all manner a Brothahs comin to yall house on Sadday an aftah Church. Hah! Cause I be lookin in yall windows when he be shootin that snotty-lookin stuff on yo faces an all up inside a yall. This yo kinda God, awright. I hopes yall *chokes* on it!" An they shet they mouths an try to ack like I be crazy. Like I don know what I be sayin. But I knowed, an it made me feel real good. Cause I unnerstood it *all* now.

An I kep walkin on toward home. When I look up, I almos fall flat on my face. Rev'ren Peach was sittin up, jes as proud as you please, on some woman front porch, talkin to her daughter. I knowed, I *swear* I knowed, that gal momma wasn home. That there gal was me. Hate for Peach, for all the "Sistahs" an "Brothahs," for my momma, it spilled all ovah me. For lettin this happen to me. To that lil gal on the front porch with Rev'ren Peach. The Rev'ren an them been fuckin up gal chirrens for a long ole time. Probly since fuckin beginned. An *evrybody* was jes as pleased as pie to let it go on. But I weren.

Nex time somebody axe me who baby it was, I say, "It yourn! An yourn! An yourn!" They faces was fixin to laugh, but they stop befo they grins git to they mouths. I look at em in they eyes. I points my fingahs at em. An they call me crazy.

When I drop my baby, they twist they faces inta somethin what spose to be a smile, an they axe, "Whacha gone name im, honey?" All smilin in my face, hopin I ain gone ac-cuse em. Hope Ima fahgive em like they Jesus spose to. But I spit at em an say, "He name Rev'ren Peach."

They faces go slack. They tries to smile, but they faces look like they cain make em work no mo. They look like they the ones what killed they Lawd Jesus. They em-barrassed.

They say, "You cain name no baby that. Sholy!?" But they says it like a question.

I say, "He name Rev'ren Peach. Like his pappy. Like *yo* baby pappy! Like *my* pappy!" I stop, cause I'm cryin. "Like he oughtta be name!"

I thought maybe they stop lettin Rev'ren Peach fuck up they girl chirrens, fuck up they daughters, fuck up they futures. But they didn. They had the white folks put me in this heah paddy cell. Where I cain brush my teeths. Where all I can heah is womens screamin an cryin. I axes em, "Is Rev'ren Peach bother you, too? If he is, Ima git im when I gits outta heah. Ima git outta heah like he done, an Ima git im back." But look like these womens cain heah me. Alls they can heah is somethin goin on all the time in they heads.

Seem like I been heah a awful long time, too. Other day, somebody tole me I been heah nigh on eight years an six months. Rev'ren Peach weren heah *nearly* this long, an I knows for *true* they was folks what burn to death when he set fire to his pappy Church. But I knows it they Lawd Will I be punish mo. Cause they Lawd say I'm a Sinnah. An a woman, to boot. An they God, He rule this worl. They God an the white folks God. One an the same. But I swears Ima git Rev'ren Peach when I gits out. Cause theys a lot a gal chirrens out theah. An evry dog, she have her day.

Dorothy Bryant

◆

Blood Relations

T HEY HAD THEIR USUAL season tickets and, when the first
play opened, Frank realized that he wanted to go. David,
back in the hospital again, encouraged him. "Take Paul, or Jay." But
Frank didn't want to see any of their friends.

There were his sisters, his parents, his cousin. No. He decided
he wanted his grandmother, who had never gone to plays and
concerts and was now over eighty, with failing sight, hearing,
memory. "Come with me, Nonna. It's a musical, *Sunday in the Park
with George.*" He knew she would come. The only grandson of a large
family, Italian on both sides, he could count on her old unjust
preference. For once he was glad of it, shameless.

They drove down Geary Street through gradually thickening
traffic. At a long stoplight, he suddenly asked her one of the old
questions about his grandfather, whom he knew only through
photographs and the stories Nonna told him. It had been years
since she'd told this one, his favorite. How he and his grandfather
were together all the time in those last months, puttering in the
garden until he was too weak. How Frank, barely three years old

but talking constantly in either English or Italian (he could not speak a word of Italian now), understood his grandfather perfectly. No one else could, not after seven operations on his cancerous jaw.

Frank's memories began after his grandfather's death, when Nonna became the settled, widowed old lady he knew. He never thought of her as ever having had a husband. He never asked her how she had endured those two years of his grandfather's terrible dying. Frank's mother said that Nonna nursed him day and night, never complained, never cried. Only that by the time he died, she had a slight tremor, an almost imperceptible shaking of her head that still remained after thirty years. It was as if she were constantly whispering inwardly, No, no, no.

♦ ♦ ♦

Frank dropped her in front of the theater while he parked the car. Alone, he felt a stab of guilt. These stabs came regularly now when, absorbed at work, he forgot for a few minutes, then suddenly remembered David sitting at home, probably staring out the garden window. Or when he took a deep breath of cool, foggy air, felt a surge of ordinary well-being, and rejoiced in it. And then remembered David with silvery-blue plastic oxygen tubes in his nose. He wondered if Nonna had ever felt guilty for not being able to share each moment of her husband's pain.

♦ ♦ ♦

He found her just where he had left her, shivering a bit in the crowd. It took them some minutes to inch their way across the jammed, noisy lobby, to squeeze into the elevator, to find their seats. The theater, filling quickly, was already hot and stuffy, and Nonna looked tired. Usually she was in bed by this time. It had been cruel to bring her. She would not enjoy this kind of musical.

Even Frank preferred the old-fashioned kind, with tunes you could hum.

She sat silent beside him, as usual. Living alone all these years, she had no one to talk to. She spent hours working jigsaw puzzles, as she had done with his grandfather during those final months. It had been something they could do without his having to talk. A visitor could join their silence, watching, fitting in a piece or two. When Frank was there, Nonna had told him, his grandfather would hand him a piece and show him how to fit it in, which he did with great concentration and satisfaction. No, he could not remember that either.

Aside from the puzzles, she read an occasional best-seller, watched television, telephoned her grandchildren. Yet even on the phone she said little. There was silence in her eyes, too. They looked, they saw, they expressed nothing. Frank was grateful for that tonight. It would have been a mistake to have brought his mother. Her eyes said everything. Whenever she looked at him, they widened into an abyss of prophecy, full of images of him in David's place. Last week, suddenly infuriated, he had snapped at her, "Don't bury me yet!" It was a strange phrase for him to use, more like something Nonna would say.

A few minutes into the play he was sure they should not have come. He did not want to sit in the dark listening to these tones of abrasive, intellectual sentiment. It would have been better if they had gone to a movie, where he could cry. Like Nonna, he never cried. Except at the movies, where sometimes, at the most banal scenes, tears suddenly spilled down his cheeks. How David laughed at him! But he had not been to a movie these past two months. The flat, simplistic images that usually relaxed and distracted him had become unbearable, torture by stupidity.

Only his job, only work brought him relief. Nonna had had no job during those two years, no break from nursing her husband, using up their savings, then going to work after he died, on night shift for the next twenty years, "not to be alone when the sun goes down." After the first week, Frank realized he was lucky that he had to go to work every day.

Lucky. It was a word he and David used often now. Lucky to have each other, not like some poor bastard all alone. Lucky to have their own house, no panicky roommates or landlord to evict them. Lucky that family, friends, employers, all were behaving well, impeccably, like Nonna who had, as usual in any family crisis, sent jars of soup, ravioli, and her incomparable veal cutlets. David had laughed and said he wondered where on the hierarchy of "luckier than they" he and Frank stood. Surely his former lovers were calling themselves lucky not to be Frank. He and David laughed a lot these days, alone together, or with friends and family. Everyone roared at each other's jokes. They had become the ideal audience for a stand-up comic, all eagerly pitched on the edge of laughter, dreading the silence that followed.

◆ ◆ ◆

Frank found himself drawn into the play in spite of, or because of, the abrasive, repetitive music. Maybe he felt in tune with this music that wasn't trying to be sweet and this story that led nowhere. Ragged and hesitant and fragmented, the story lurched from side to side rather than forward, as George, the impressionist artist, conceived his painting from the bits and pieces of his life, fitting them together into beauty no one else could see.

Frank wondered if Nonna was paying attention or daydreaming. Could she follow the play? Or did she see and hear and then forget a moment later, as she forgot so many things now? How much did she actually understand before she forgot? Did she understand what was happening to David and would possibly—probably— happen to Frank? He stopped that thought, grabbed it, firmly put it aside. Stopping thought was a new process for him, requiring great discipline. Maybe Nonna didn't really forget, but had learned to put aside certain thoughts she must live with.

♦ ♦ ♦

When the houselights came up for intermission, she nodded, yes, she was enjoying the play. No, she did not want to leave her seat. She sat watching people move about. Frank knew she would not speak again unless he asked her a question. "Did you ever get mad at my grandfather, I mean when he was sick?"

She seemed unsurprised by the question, nodding as if always ready with the answer. "At the end, the last months, when he was leaving me."

Frank nodded. It had come sooner to him, the rage, and to David as well. Anger exploded in small ways, in telephoning from work and yelling when he learned that David would not, could not, eat his lunch. In low, petty ways, like his sulking when David called the AIDS Project to ask for a counselor, someone who would "come between us," Frank whined, flinching at the contempt in David's eyes, in his cutting response, and then, worst of all, in his silence. They apologized, forgave, quarreled again, made up, forgave, wondered at the ignoble form their anguish took. They were not prepared for this, they who had prepared so well.

They had been together five years when the blood test became available, and they took it, glad of the chance to escape the cloud hanging over their friends, confident that their fiercely defended monogamy would be vindicated. They could hardly believe the results. Positive. Each had picked up the virus years ago. Or one had carried it to the other.

They made their wills, took vitamins, went to bed early, stopped drinking even wine, talked about death-with-dignity, quoted statistics. Only ten percent of positives got sick. Twenty percent. Thirty-five to forty percent. The statistics changed as the year slowly passed, until David became a statistic.

Now their suicide pact was revealed as childish romanticism. Their contempt for heroic measures shriveled and, abjectly, they accepted medical assault. Dignity dissolved in the ocean of petty necessities—the unwashed dishes, the disability application, the mortgage payments—the dozens of reminders that, while everyone must die, life lurches on.

♦ ♦ ♦

The lights dimmed again. Now the setting was modern, and the great-grandson of George was the artist, still struggling with the same questions, his own life a fragmented puzzle. The baby in the first-act painting was now a grandmother, dozing and drooping in a wheelchair, singing in a weak, piping squeak, "Children and art, children and art."

Frank waited to see if the insistent chant of that simple equation would take him in like a movie and wet his eyes, but it did not touch him. He would never have children, and he didn't make art. Whatever he left would not be so easy to name. What did Nonna think of that song? Not children and art, just children. They were all that mattered to Nonna. That was why she was here with him, why she would sit in the dark through anything with him. So, the force that held them together was, in reality, a huge gap between them. Did she even know him? Did she understand why he needed her tonight, needed to begin to learn what she had known for thirty years?

He reached out to take her hand, gently, respectful of her arthritis. She gave his hand a quick, hard squeeze. Her strength surprised him, hurt him. She had never been so abrupt with him, so rough. He had never felt so grateful. They sat and watched the rest of the play, hand in hand, dry eyed, two old soldiers in the long war.

Marnie Mueller

◆

What Would You Have Done?

ANDREAS AND I are in the living room reading the Sunday
New York Times. It's a rainy day and the heavy downpour is
drumming incessantly on the skylight.

"Do you know what the White Rose is?" I ask.

"Why?" He looks up, his blond hair haloed by the overhead
table light.

"There's a review of a movie about it."

"It was a resistance group of university students during the war.
In Munich."

"How did you know about it?"

"Everybody knows that." His blue eyes harden. "They're national
heroes in Germany." He goes back to reading the newspaper.

This area has been sensitive for us throughout our fifteen years
together. On the first day I met Andreas, I asked him what his
family had done during the war and he told me his father had been
a member of the Nazi Party. We were walking along the water's
edge at Southampton Beach.

"You know I'm Jewish," I said. I am Jewish on my mother's side, although my name, Caitlin Saunders, gives no hint of it.

"No, I didn't."

"What do you say to it?"

"Nothing." He kept walking without looking at me.

"What would you have done in your father's place?" I asked defiantly.

"Probably the same thing." He stopped walking. He crossed his arms over his bare chest and stared at me. The corners of his mouth turned down. "He had a family to protect and provide for.'

Early in our marriage I used to harangue him about his father. Karl Schmidt died when Andreas was only fourteen so he never had a chance to ask any of the necessary questions. I would say he should ask his mother. I would couch it in terms that it would be good for him. Andreas has never gotten over his father's death; to this day he will weep for him on Christmas Eve. His father died shortly before Christmas and as the only male left in the family, Andreas had to read the story of the birth of Christ to his grieving mother and sisters. I would say to him that half the reason he never got over it was that he was afraid of what his father had done. I was vicious in those fights. I would push him until he clammed up and then I would rush over him with words. The more words I poured out, the more silent he became. Until I would punch him to get a response, and pull his hair and he would curl and crouch to get away from me. Only once did he strike back and that was a sideways glance of his foot to my ankle. I stopped attacking him after he fought back, and since then, every time we speak of things German or Jewish, we're careful.

We walk across Central Park. The rain has stopped. The grass and leaves are electric green in the evening light, and the cherry trees on 72nd Street are in full pink bloom. I am nervous, though, that we aren't going to get into the movie. When we arrive at Fifth Avenue, I talk Andreas into taking a taxi the rest of the way. He agrees, but says, "I don't think we have to worry. Not so many people are interested in seeing a movie about heroic Germans."

He's right. When we arrive twenty minutes before the movie is to begin, there's a line of ten people. I'm almost embarrassed to join them, but do, with the same determination I've used in the past to march in a demonstration of a few hundred, when I know I can be singled out.

We wait, eating apples and making small talk. By the time we go in, the line has grown to only fifty ticket holders.

The film begins with a young university woman being greeted in the train station in Munich by her brother. The moment they open their mouths it's apparent they're speaking in Swabian dialect. They sound exactly like Andreas. They could be Andreas and his sister Beate. It's a soft, free way of speaking, nothing like the parodies of Germans that people usually do. I wonder if the audience can tell the difference. I suspect not.

The movie proceeds in simple terms. Everyday terms. Only occasionally is there a brown shirt in evidence or a swastika. But you feel the presence begin to mount. You gradually see what these young people were up against and in the end you realize how naive and foolhardy they were, especially when the screen goes black and the whack of the guillotine is heard as it slices off the Resistance girl's head.

When the lights come up, I say to Andreas, "I think it was quite good. I don't know what the reviewers meant when they said it was amateurish." But he sits forward as though to get away from me and I'm embarrassed. I want to apologize, to say something to make up for my trivial comment, but nothing comes to mind. After a while I reach out and take his hand. To my relief he clutches it tightly.

By the time we get up to leave most of the people are in the aisles, walking slowly and silently, as though leaving a church. As we make our way along the row, I hear weeping. I look back into the dim theatre and see a couple sitting in the center of all the empty seats. The man has his arms completely around the woman.

Her head is in his chest and she is crying hysterically, almost to a wail. The man has a dark beard. I have no idea what she looks like, but her weeping enters me and for the first time, I fill with tears.

We walk along the packed East Side street. Crowds are waiting to get into the latest best-selling movie. Andreas announces that he doesn't want to eat anything. I flare up inside. It's an old story. He withholds by not wanting to go to dinner.

"That's all right," I say, "but maybe we could get something to take out. We have nothing at home."

He doesn't answer me. I hold back my growing rage. All my sympathy in the theatre has turned to old resentment. Why can't he deal directly with what he's feeling? Why can't he talk about it? We walk along, bumping into people. Punkers. Green haired kids all in black. Washed out white faces. A boy eating fire for money. We get to the corner. Bloomingdale's is across the street. The avenue is clogged with cars. We hesitate. I don't know what to do. Should we walk until we get out of this unappealing crowd? Should we catch a bus? I want to eat, damn it. I look over at Andreas, ready to scream at him that he'd better decide what to do since he's the one who doesn't want to eat, when I see his face. It's pale with panic. His thin neck has gone scrawny. He looks about to pass out or vomit.

"Andreas, liebling," comes out of me. I touch his clammy forehead. "I'll find us a cab."

In the taxi, after I've given the driver our address, Andreas leans back against the seat, his body slack, his head lolling to one side.

"I have such a headache," he says. "It must be the air."

"When did it start?"

"In the movie."

"You don't think it had to do with the movie?"

"No, it was the air. It was so close."

I don't argue with him. Instead, I put my arm around his shoulder and pull him to me. He comes willingly. He lets his head drop down onto my breast. I put my other hand over his face. I hold him like that as the cab races and bumps and careens along the Central Park transverse at 66th Street. I'm surprised he allows this. I love the feeling of cradling him. He is a child and I'm his protector. It makes me feel strong.

Riding up Central Park West, he sits up and smiles at me.

"Thanks, I feel better."

"Is the headache gone?"

"No, but I don't feel so sick. Maybe I'd like to eat something after all."

We talk about nothing much through our beers and hamburgers in a neighborhood pub. Only after the waiter has brought the check does Andreas' face grow sad again.

"You know," he says, "I wrote a poem about the White Rose once." I can see how difficult this is for him to say.

"Did you write it when you were a student in the university in Munich?"

He nods, his mouth tight with emotion.

"Did you imagine you were one of them, handing out leaflets on the campus?"

"Yes," he says, in a whisper.

Louise Rafkin

♦

Blueprints for
Modern Living

This period is only a historical accident.
—*Isabel Allende*

The Earth's Rotation

I WAKE FEELING as though I am in the belly of a giant whale. I lie still in my bed, braced for a toss and a tumble, unsure. The rolling stops and I sit up on my elbows, queasy from seasickness, or not enough sleep. The house groans, starts rumbling and I realize: another earthquake.

Watching the lights sway, I think about standing under a door frame but instead my gaze is drawn to a print, framed and under glass, directly above my pillow. I've considered moving it, imagining it crashing upon me in the midst of The Big One. The day after an earthquake the papers are splashed with predictions. "Scientists Say Big Quake Overdue" or, depending on the paper, "Disaster Imminent!" I gave up reading those articles and I've never read Jeanne Dixon's yearly forecasts in the *Enquirer*. It's not that I think they're a sham, or hokey, or even scientifically unsound; it's just that at this point in my life I'll gladly trade surety for a sense of possibility, even if that possibility spells disaster.

The print does not fall yet I imagine my obituary: "The deceased survived by. . ." Who? Whom am I survived by? We all survive because we all survive—it's not poetic, I know. But given that when we all go—whether it's because of that black hole spreading across the ozone or because our man in D.C. decides to show them Ruskies who's boss—we'll all go together. Individual deaths aren't of interest anymore, they hardly make the news. The day of this earthquake we all survive, every last one of us mad enough to live on this lovable fault we call home.

The neighborhood dogs begin their morning a cappella concert. I do not go outside; I do not start to bottle water; I do not switch off the gas. No, I turn on the television and learn I—and all of us—have lived through a medium-sized tremor, four-something on Mr. Richter's scale. I expect we'll watch the world's grand finale on Good Morning America. Will Bryant Gumbel sign off for us all? A few aftershocks murmur under my bare feet like the faint waves of pleasure after orgasm. I climb back into my still toasty bed, masturbate and fall back asleep. And the phone rings.

"You all right?" It is my mother calling from Florida. "Alison? Honey?"

"I'm fine. It was just a small one."

She calls every time there's an earthquake, incredulous that I live in California, which she is sure will soon join Hawaii in the Pacific Ocean. I, however, am appalled that she lives in Florida, where each year she gets friendly with a hurricane and for weeks calls it by name. "Flora is still on her way," she assures me as if Flora was dropping in for a cup of tea. She lives through hurricanes, my sister in Oregon lives through ice storms, I live through earthquakes. We all make our choices, I suppose, based on what we can endure.

Somehow I prefer my disaster to come from below, from the shifting of the world's crusty plates; Ma Kettle's indigestion.

"I've got to go to work, Mom." I lie. However, she readily agrees to get off the phone. Long distance is a modern extravagance she has never fully accepted. I have seen her phone bill; each long distance entry is noted—after the number and price is a word, the cause for the call. Last time I visited I watched her make these markings; "Birthday" she wrote under a call to my sister in Oregon, "Death" she scratched over a Michigan entry. I can imagine her penciling in the word "Earthquake" alongside my Berkeley number.

The Day's Rotation

Hardly anyone talks about the earthquake for the rest of the day. It's Saturday and I meet my friend Lenny at a cafe because we've decided to go to a protest together. Sometimes I read about New York where people of our age (that age right before thirty when all is not possible nor even probable anymore) meet at gallery openings or rock clubs and put more up their noses in a half hour than Lenny and I make in a day. In Berkeley we meet at bookstores or protests, or over cappucino in one of the many cafes near the university. Walking between the divided lots of people on historic Telegraph Avenue—the street people, flanked by dogs, army packs and shopping bags, and the young, optimistic, selectively-sighted university students dressed in bright colors harsh against the gray and luminous sky—we slip invisibly into anonymity. Here, next to the polluted San Francisco Bay, guarded by the picture-perfect Golden Gate Bridge, we live lives undocumented by the media; somewhere between yuppies and hippies we latent members of the baby boom drive around the pot-holed, palm-tree-lined streets of California in Valiants and old Volvos trying, unsuccessfully and without validation, to place our lives into historical context.

Lenny and I work at a newspaper, a lefty sort of newspaper, and we set type which is a romantic way of saying that we sit in front of computer terminals and get paid twice as much as secretaries for essentially the same work. Lenny is very good at it, which means he understands exactly how the machine unravels the commands we punch in. I don't understand the machine and when faced with a problem usually start pressing buttons indiscriminately in the hopes of controlling what I sense is an arbitrary electronic process. About once a week I lose entire stories as a result of my impatience with computer logic—and where they go I've no idea. I'll be working along, talking with Lenny about the Faulkner book he's been reading, or about my girlfriend, or about his marriage breaking up, and then while reaching for my coffee I'll brush the keyboard and the whole thing vanishes. Poof! It has to do with "appending" and "replacing" and I try to keep very concrete pictures in my head of old-fashioned file cabinets so as to do the right one at the right time. But as I say, the machine usually wins and eats the story just as I've finished typing it in. It's usually something long and boring about parking, or city politics, or a letter to the editor about dog shit on our streets and then I have to gear up to start all over, or take a coffee break. I'm not a good typesetter but it's a union shop and they'd have a hard time getting rid of me. Sometimes that's the irony of leftist organizing: if I was stuck with me as a typesetter I'd think twice about unions.

Lenny is sitting at the cafe drinking black coffee out of a pint-sized styrofoam cup and eating a dry bagel. He's been dieting ever since his wife left him. Actually, she didn't leave him, she said she needed some space and then bought it. They got married six years ago after knowing each other for three months, a leap of faith in the best of times but in those days it must have been fueled by fervent and illogical hope. Marriage and commitment have gained popularity over the last few years, but Lenny got married at a time when anything more than living together seemed like a throwback to the fifties. He believes in marriage, in love, and in some ways, justice. Coupled with his devotion to good books, this is what makes Lenny interesting to me. I, who at twelve could not fathom what was described to me as the Holocaust: I, who in my early twenties truly believed the ERA would pass and who at twenty-eight could not begin to understand the minds who not only thought up such a plan as Star Wars, but had the audacity to start building space shields: I found myself rooting for Lenny's marriage with the zeal of a high-school cheerleader. It's an interesting alliance, Lenny and I, one my girlfriend and his wife—possibly ex-wife—are just beginning to understand; friendship between a straight man and a lesbian is rare, even in Berkeley.

"Hey, skinny," I say, pulling up a chair and setting my salmon covered bagel on the coffee-stained table. Lenny sits hunched over the morning newspaper, his well-worn jean jacket on the chair beside him, his white, button-down shirt tucked into a pair of deep blue—new, I suppose—Levi 501s. Lenny's hair looks as if it houses a family of mice; falling well below his ears, his brown, fine curls often cover his eyes. Sometimes when he typesets he'll take one hand and brush the hair from his forehead, sometimes when it isn't there. He's still a faster typist than me, even with that one hand waving about.

"Hey," Lenny says, looking up.

"What's news?" I ask.

The front page of the paper is covered with photographs, a frame-by-frame account of a train in the act of running over an anti-war protester. Against my intentions I find myself scrutinizing the photos, looking for an expression on the engineer's face that will explain something to me, looking for a sign that would signify why god would allow another atrocity. All I see is a child, holding his head with both hands as his stepfather loses both legs, and a bride of eight days rushing to her husband's side trying to hold blood within her husband's body with only the torn hem of her skirt.

"Did you feel the earthquake?" I ask, tearing my eyes away from the paper. I feel slightly nauseous thinking about the man's foot, severed and autonomous, lying on the railroad tracks, discarded and limp like a day-old newspaper. I move the lox across the table.

"I slept right though it," he says through a bite of his bagel. We sit there for a moment; Lenny chewing, me thinking about him sleeping through the quake. He grew up in California, in one of those cities clustered around Los Angeles that all seem the same to me, in a home not unlike mine, though mine sat in a similar suburb in Michigan. Our parents are middle-class, Christian, Republican. They watched us grow up safely in the chasm between the sixties and drugs, and the eighties and money. Coming of age in the seventies was like being in that middle part of the tennis court my father calls "no man's land": too far forward to catch balls at the baseline, too far back to play the net. I watched my older sister smoke pot in the garage, protest Vietnam on television, live with a succession of men, arrange at least two abortions and survive a number of "bad trips." Is this what I missed by being born too late? Now, she is married to a schoolteacher and is raising two sons in a small city in Oregon. On weekends she and Rick, now her husband after eight years of being her 'man,' pile the kids into an old station wagon and pull a small egg-shaped trailer to the country where they fish and, when the kids fall asleep, smoke tightly rolled joints. I think this is what Lenny had expected for himself and his bride, Kate. But Kate decided to go into computers, started making big money and thus: her own condo overlooking the bay, complete with a creamy leather couch and pink levolors. Lenny lives in their old place, a rented cottage in a quirky neighborhood below the university. He kept their record collection; Kate uprooted the herb garden and took it, potted, to her condo. "Can't live without my basil," she said. Lenny now calls her "The Pesto Queen."

There is not much to say about the morning's news.

"How's Maggie?" Lenny says, and I say "Fine" even though there's a lot I could say. There is a way being friends with Lenny has got built-in safety catches, for both of us. It's not going to be complicated by matters of love or lust, and the way that we don't know the realities of each others' lives keeps everything so safe. Sometimes, guiltily, I feel like I'm looking at Lenny through Wild Kingdom glasses, like he's a rare bird and I'm documenting his mating patterns.

"Kate's seeing José," he adds.

"Seeing, or seeing," I ask.

"Sleeping with."

"That explains the Spanish language course," I say and laugh and immediately regret it.

"Thanks," he says into his coffee.

I try to redeem myself. "She's a jerk."

He smiles. He's got these doe-like eyes, moist and soft and his right hand gracefully flutters across his forehead sweeping the hair from his head. I'm forgiven. I vow not to be so coarse; I want people like Lenny in my life.

"Let's go," he says.

I wrap my bagel in a paper napkin and stick it in the pocket of my tattered leather jacket. We are going to the train tracks where the man was run over.

At the Edge of the Tide

Inland, the windless country is dry and hot. We leave our jackets in my old red Valiant and join the crowds of people walking toward the weapons station. I bought the Valiant from my sister when she left for college years ago, for the fair and reasonable sum of five hundred dollars. In high school and later in college, kids laughed at my red beast; such a tank, such an old folks' car, they'd say. Over the past few years—thanks to the union—I've given her a new paint job, reupholstered her seats, cleaned up her original engine. Now I am offered substantial amounts of money for her by the same people who laughed me out of the high school parking lot. "Wannasell?" they'll ask me from within their Honda civics. "Fat chance," I spit back, my voice betraying some bitterness. Besides, I had my first girl in the back seat, Carrie Sue Thomas, after the Homecoming game senior year. My mother recently reported that Carrie Sue is married and selling real estate in St. Paul.

There are hundreds going to protest: old, young, families carrying picnics, dogs on and off leashes. As we approach the site, we are accosted by all forms of fliers thrust at us like the arms of turnstiles at the grocery store: brightly colored sheets of paper covered by type so dense they're less inviting than a Republican fundraiser. Each splinter of every communist or socialist group tries to pass its party line to the already converted masses as if the protest was a revival meeting and they are fighting for our lost souls. Both Lenny and I keep our hands deep in our pockets and shake our head at every invitation. I spot a woman I know who works at a large multinational; she is wearing a long black wig and passing out leaflets for the Marxist-Leninists. I'm sure she doesn't want to be recognized and I'm glad I can slip by her flailing arms without recognition.

A stage is set up near the train tracks, hay has been spread on the dirt and the lines for the Porta-Johns are already twenty deep. From this small spot on the dry California landscape our military ships guns and missiles to Nicaragua, the Persian Gulf, and who knows where else? First they—and when I say "they" I can only think of faceless, clean-shaven young men, both black and white (indistinguishable in their mottled army fatigues), sweat dripping from their temples under our warm winter sun—they load them onto trains, such as the train that ran over the now legless man. They are driven to the sea and make their way to the Pacific Slipping silently under the Golden Gate Bridge, the weapons—the guns and missiles and whatever else is packed in those crates marked boldly for the world to see—become our offering to the peoples of this planet.

Lenny is unusually silent. He sits down between the Gray Panthers and the Vietnam vets. I cannot think of a more perfect place to sit: between inspiration and hope. The vets stand at attention, mirrored sunglasses cover emotion, worn jeans poke out from beneath flak jackets or ribboned and bejeweled military coats Pony tails snake down the backs of two men holding the ends of a purple and gold fringed banner: "Vietnam Veterans Opposed to U.S. Militarism." Against all intellect, my heart swells. For a moment I feel like an unmarried gal in the streets of New York on V-Day; I want to jump up and kiss the tall, lanky stranger on my left, hungry for that bravery to rub off upon my lips! Yet I can't help but think of them as both brave and foolish as if they have taken a hairpin turn on Highway 1 on a rainy and wet, black winter's night—and come out laughing, bleary-eyed, tears tracking the crevices of their cheeks.

The gray-haired woman to my right looks not unlike my mother, save for a "U.S. Out of Central America" button pinned to the collar of her polyester shell. She is passing fried chicken to her friends, pouring coffee from a red thermos; Lenny and I have brought a pint of mineral water and two Hershey bars. I imagine her frying that chicken early in the morning, wrapping it in Saran Wrap and placing each piece in a Tupperware box, like any woman preparing for a picnic, a car trip—a protest? The man I think is her husband clasps a clipboard to his chest, a petition that he offers me and that I sign without reading. I am convinced that whatever this couple believes in, I must believe in too. I smile and hand the clipboard back to him. "Thanks," I say and the woman offers me a serene smile between sips of coffee. The domesticity of the scene has not escaped Lenny's notice; he takes the clipboard and signs his name to the list of believers and I suspect both of us want to ask the same questions: How did you get this far together? How do you keep believing?

Riding Out the Current

Lenny is weeping, quietly, on the passenger's side of the Valiant on the way back from the protest. The protest was successful, I suppose, in numerical terms. And Joan Baez sang the Lord's Prayer and Jesse Jackson got us to stand, hands clasped and raised against the glaring sun. I'm driving and talking about time. I am interested in the way people visualize life on those picture screens in our heads. And I'm nervous about Lenny crying.

"In my mind life looks like a series of building blocks, only there are turns at certain points," I try to explain. I trace a path along the inside of the dirty windshield and Lenny wipes his eyes and looks at the snakelike diagram.

"Here's birth," I point to the near end of the snake. "Then there's this curve around to here, that's about ten years old, and then there's this long stretch here that reaches to thirty." I glance at Lenny and I see that he's stopped crying and has pulled his hair down over his brow so I can hardly see his eyes; I'm sure he doesn't want me to see him cry and I'm not sure I want to anyway. "I'm just at this turn, here, and then I slide over the hill and down to forty. How does a life look in your mind?"

I've always been interested in how people organize concepts in their heads. I have another diagram in my head for the twenty-four hours of the day which has similar curves and twists to the life-snake. I have a blimp-like picture in my mind for the seven days of the week, and a strange "D" pattern for the year which inexplicably gives extra space to the summer months. Maggie, my girlfriend, says she has no organizing patterns for time and watching her live I am apt to believe her. With the turn of thirty before me, I am more interested than ever in these mental blueprints.

Lenny doesn't answer me. Instead he starts to cry again, full force.

"Don't cry," I say foolishly and try to merge with oncoming traffic while watching Lenny's chest heave and rock. "Everything will work out." This is something I hear on bad TV movies and I am somewhat shocked to hear me say it. I've never seen Lenny cry like this before, in fact have never seen a man cry like this ever. Crying women sound like small captured animals, raspy with sharp noises coming from somewhere in the back of their throats. Lenny sounds like a harpooned whale; bursts of long and low pitched sound come up from his belly. He's crying harder and louder and I am frantic trying to figure out what to do, what to say, how to stay within the white lines of the freeway and the cool corridors of our friendship. Pulling off at the first exit, I drive into the parking lot of a giant Safeway. I park the Valiant alongside a recycling trailer and Lenny doubles over his knees; his head touches the dash.

Slowly, I slide over the front seat and place one hand across Lenny's wide back. His body rises and falls as he tries to regain his breath. My touch is light, but I can feel warmth coming through his shirt.

"Lenny?" I ask. "Hey, Lenny?"

His back falls one more time and he straightens up in the car. My hand is pinned between him and the seat. And then I see his face, twisted and tight, and his red, puffy eyes and I begin to cry. And I am crying for Lenny because his wife isn't going to come back to him, and I reckon even if she did he wouldn't want her. And I'm crying because losing two legs is both too much and too little in this war we are waging against the world. And I'm crying because I'm about to turn that corner in my mind and slide over thirty and I have no career, no babies, no husband, no picket fence. And now Lenny is holding me, and I him and though I haven't held a man since 1979 when my father and I went camping and he turned his ankle and I had to carry him through the forest, this holding seems as natural as apple pie and ice cream. Twice the size of Maggie, Lenny rests against my chest with the weight of a wall of water. Both of us are crying.

Shoring Up

I left Lenny at a cafe where he was meeting a friend. There was something new between us, a sadness and a hope, as if we had jointly lived through a crisis or disaster, though whatever happened to each of us that day happened quite separately as well as together. I drove to Maggie's house where she was busy at the stove concocting a kind of goulash. I ate heartily, mounds of potatoes and carrots, sopping up the brown gravy with huge hunks of sour bread. After dinner I planned my own birthday party, making long lists of guests and supplies. I don't want to be alone when I turn that corner.

That night there was another earthquake, smaller than the one that morning. They called it an aftershock. I wondered if Lenny slept through that one, too.

Deborah Rose O'Neal

◆

Marguerite Marie

"**A**RE YOU WORRIED?" asked Blue.

"No," answered Marguerite Marie. "For the one hundredth time, I am *not* worried. I am definitely not worried. No."

"Come on, Ems, not even a little bit worried?" asked Blue.

Blue was making angel wings in the sand with her nicely rounded white feet. She wasn't looking into her sister's eyes and Marguerite Marie was glad of that.

"No," said Marguerite, crumpling and releasing the nylon ruffle on the edge of her magenta swimsuit. "Not even a little. Don't you remember the night she left us off at the movies and didn't come back till two shows later? That was sure longer than this."

Blue stopped moving her angel feet.

"Yeah," she said, "and that time she gave us a dollar each in case we needed food or a bus home. This time she only gave us fifty cents each for ice cream."

Marguerite clenched her fist inside her sweatshirt pocket. Her hand was gritty with sand and sweat.

"Right," said Marguerite Marie because it was the older sister's job to be very sure, just like it was the younger sister's job to ask the scary questions and expect answers that made her feel warm and good inside. Even if the sisters were only half sisters. And even if the older sister was only twelve years old. And even if the sweat on the hand of the older sister was the sweat of worry and fear and not the sweat of the afternoon heat of the beach.

"I'm going in," announced Blue.

"Wait, hide your quarters in your shoe."

Blue tossed them into the toe of her transparent pink jelly shoes, and ran off toward the water, her golden legs pumping, spitting sand behind.

"You stay right in front of me while you're swimming, you hear?"

Blue let her arms fly out, hands waving, to say she had heard.

Marguerite slid along the bed quilt that served as the girls' beach blanket. It was a picture quilt made by Marguerite's black granny somewhere in Louisiana, and it showed a farmhouse and a tree and a man and a lady on the top half. On the bottom were rows of brown sticks with white puffs attached to the tops and black people with colorful pieces of material on their heads, standing beside the brown sticks. Momma had thrown the quilt into a closet when Granny first sent it, and later used it, decoration side down, as a rug for everyone to walk on. Marguerite had taken it to the laundromat one day, washed it clean, brought it home and hid it till Momma promised to let her have it for herself.

"Why you want to be reminded of your black half by sleeping under that thing is beyond me," her mother had said. "You'd think the mirror would be enough."

"Then why'd you let him be my daddy?" Marguerite had yelled, clutching the quilt so that she wouldn't topple over from anger.

"Pure mistake. All the more because it made for your poor sister, Josephine, being born blue. It doesn't ever do to mix, Marguerite Marie. Oh, if I could start over, if only your poor mother could start over right now and forever..."

Marguerite reached for Blue's two quarters. The jelly shoes had grown hot in the sun. They smelled like new tar, laid down in wide, healing sweeps on a summer blacktop. Someone could slip the coins right out of those shoes, steal them clean. Marguerite pushed the coins into the toe of her right sneaker, placed her own two quarters into her left sneaker, rolled her sweatshirt up, and set it, pocket side to the quilt. Then, she unfolded her long, dark legs and scanned the ocean. Blue was hopping around in the water with what looked like a family. Two kids younger than Blue, about five and seven, and a father playing monster, playing whale, playing man under the bed.

Marguerite kept a sharp, curious eye on him. What kind of a man would hang around with the children he fathered when he could be off seeing the world like her daddy? Like Blue's daddy? Marguerite walked down toward the water. She held onto the ruffle of her bathing suit, rolling it between her fingers, letting it unfurl, quick as a whisper, and then forcing it into a slick curl again.

She saw the man smiling at Blue, lifting her up and up into the air. It seemed like Blue was part of his family now, instead of belonging with her own sister.

"Josephine!" shouted Marguerite. "You get out, now."

Blue looked over at Marguerite. So did the man.

"Who's that?" he asked. "Your nanny?" He opened his mouth wide when he laughed.

That was how Momma let it be known sometimes. By a quiet "No, not *both* of them," in response to a curious stranger. Sometimes by even less than that. By a turn of the eye, twist of the neck in denial. People were ready to believe that Marguerite Marie couldn't belong, because she shouldn't belong.

Blue frowned, pinching in her skin frosted with hair so light it could hardly be defined as an eyebrow. To Marguerite's satisfaction, she saw the defiance and loyalty roll in across Blue's features and put up her mouth.

"She's my sister," said Blue. "Come to tell me my mother's waiting for us."

Blue stomped through the last few feet of water to the shore, raising lacy ruffles of sea water around her ankles. Everything Blue did came out beautiful.

If Marguerite could have chosen one thing to be, it would have been beautiful. Momma always said if you weren't born rich, you had to be either beautiful or smart to make your way, and that, for a woman, beautiful was better. Like Eva, who lived upstairs from them and was an executive secretary to a very important man, downtown. Eva bought her clothes according to what was new these days and she fitted her body to them like taffy into wrappers Eva's gold frosted hair curled itself long and slow, not short and skimpy, and she said she could use any office machine in the world that any man could explain to her once. A beautiful and important executive secretary was everything Marguerite ever wanted to be, even though English and Spelling were impossible mysteries to her, and clothes, no matter how new, seemed to hang like bed sheets across her bones.

"Is she back yet?" Blue asked.

"Not yet."

"Ems, I'm worried again."

"Don't, please," said Marguerite. "Let's use our ice cream money now."

"I wanna go back in. It's fun."

"No, you're not. No." Marguerite set her mouth the way she remembered Momma doing it, pulling the corners up and wide apart like an elastic band, shaking her head in a warning like the high branches of a tree just beginning to move in a storm wind.

Blue thumped her pearly toes into the sand.

"I'm going."

"You are *not*." Marguerite grabbed at Blue's fine blond curls with her dark, thin hand. She gave the curls a tug.

"You will *listen!*"

Marguerite felt lines of heat move up her hand as Blue scratched it hard. Marguerite let go, raising her hand to strike, but she forced her arm down instead, and hit her own leg with a smack that swelled and stung, absorbing heat from the air around.

"You are not my Momma!" yelled Blue.

"When Momma is gone, I am your Momma," Marguerite shouted. "And you will come along with me."

Blue mumbled something, but she started moving toward the store which occupied the bottom floor of the big white house with dark green shutters at the edge of the beach. She ambled ahead like a horse, trotting quickly for a moment, then bending her knees, dragging her feet in the sand, and trotting again, sulky and disgruntled.

Marguerite didn't care how her sister came along, as long as she did.

"I'm pretending I'm walking through fairy dust," Blue sang. "And every step is a wish and every wish is a bird and every bird flies to Momma on her bus to wherever she is going and tells her to come back to us."

Marguerite was wishing that she could wish like Blue instead of living in the air she lived in, that thundered dangers at her. She wished she didn't know that wishes don't turn into birds and that people can come to an end of things.

"If Momma's on some bus, it's taking her to Penney's to get a new blouse or to the Stop and Shop to get us some hot dogs for supper," said Marguerite.

"Did she give you any more money than fifty cents?"

"No," said Marguerite. "She did not."

"I'm getting a lime popsicle, then."

"It'll only drip green all over your legs and be gone in three minutes in the sun. I'm getting a small Coke so I can sip it all afternoon."

"You're smart," said Blue, but Marguerite knew that Blue would get the lime popsicle anyhow, and then beg for the last sip of *her* Coke, later on. And get it, too.

Mr. D'Angelo kept all sorts of treasures in his store at the edge of the beach. He had seashell bracelets and glass balls filled with water that sprinkled sequins on a lighthouse when you tipped it. He had decks of cards as small as matchbooks and pieces of coral in pinks and greens and boxes made of cedar wood that said Rock Point Beach on them in black letters, and small, polished stones for a nickel apiece. Sometimes Mr. D'Angelo gave out free pieces of bubble gum to the kids. Marguerite never accepted his gifts. She would whisper to Blue about candy and strangers, but Blue would turn her face away just enough so as not to be able to read her sister's warnings. Blue would thank Mr. D'Angelo sweetly. Marguerite tried not to like Mr. D'Angelo, but she always felt like smiling at him, and staying in his house-store a moment longer and asking him to offer her the gum so many times that she would have to accept it.

"Well, hello, girls," he said when he saw them. He had been straightening out the piles of baseball cards that the boys had left a mess. Mr. D'Angelo gave a little bow, so that Marguerite could see the bald spot on the very top of his head, sitting like a full moon in a gray sky. He was wearing a yellow shirt decorated with turquoise palm trees which stood under pink suns. Underneath tan shorts, his chubby legs squirted out and down, stuffed at the ends into brown leather sandals. Mr. D'Angelo looked the way Marguerite imagined Santa Claus would look on summer vacation.

"Today is a good luck day," said Mr. D'Angelo. He scratched the very top of his head with the tip of his little finger, waiting for the girls to respond.

"Why do you always scratch right on top?" asked Blue.

"Do I? I guess to make sure my head is still there."

Blue laughed, shrugging her shoulders and pointing her chin up at him.

"So, girls, do you need some good luck?"

"Oh, yes," said Blue, shaking her head as though it sat like a plaster doll's head on a spring. "We need *extra* good luck because..."

Marguerite caught one of the bouncing curls and pulled it.

Mr. D'Angelo turned his head toward Marguerite and straightened up. The two were of similar height, she, thin and tall, he plump and short.

"Well, Little Momma. Your baby almost told a tale? Hmmm? Are you girls in trouble?"

"No," said Marguerite, trying not to look him in the eye. She rolled the ruffle on her suit, letting it out, rolling it in, afraid he would see, underneath the fearless glaze of her dark eyes, the tears forming, ready to burst their crystal shapes and fill out into hot, plump drops that would give her away.

"Yes," said Blue. "Yes, we are. Our mother is gone."

"What?!"

"She's lying," said Marguerite. "She's not gone. It's just that Josephine had a fight with her this morning and Momma always talks about starting over and everything, especially when we have a fight. She dreams about what it would be like without us to weigh her down, what wonderful chances she would have and now Josephine feels bad about the fight, that's all."

"Are you sure?" Mr. D'Angelo leaned in towards Marguerite, who backed away an equal distance.

"She just went shopping for our supper," Marguerite continued. "Could I please have a small Coke?"

Before she could protest, Marguerite felt Mr. D'Angelo slip one of the small, polished stones into her hand.

"Free today," he said. "For good luck."

Marguerite closed her hand around the cool, smooth piece. She wanted that feeling at the center of herself.

"Where do you live?" Blue asked. She tugged on his Hawaiian shirt.

"Right here. On the top of this store is my house."

"Do you have any children?"

"Oh, yes, but they're all grown up now, and they have houses of their own to live in."

"Josephine Emily! If you dare to ask another question, you will not get to use your money this afternoon at all!"

Blue turned her face away from Marguerite's.

"May I have a lime popsicle, please?"

Mr. D'Angelo slipped a good luck stone into Blue's hand as well, and took a lime popsicle from the big, square freezer at the back of the store. He handed Marguerite her Coke.

"That's ninety-five cents all together."

Marguerite dropped the four quarters into his hand.

"Please keep the extra five cents to pay for my good luck stone.'

"It was a gift, Little Momma. It will hurt my feelings."

Marguerite was already leading the dripping Blue out of the store.

"That way," she called over her shoulder, "it will really be mine.'

"She's not coming back this time," said Blue, as they walked back to the quilt. "We have to figure out something to do."

"Don't sit on my quilt till you've finished your popsicle. Then go wash off all the sticky stuff."

"She's not coming back. Admit it." Blue licked at the chartreuse rivers that ran like veins across the top of her hand.

"She told us to wait for her and that's what we're going to do," said Marguerite, focusing on her sister again. "How about if I go to the top of the beach every half hour and meet the buses that come."

"I have my own plan." Blue twirled her sticky green index finger in her gold curls the way she always did when she was proud of herself. "I'm going to baby-sit little kids for a quarter or a dime so their Mommas can go in swimming. Then we can get hamburgs or hot dogs at Mr. D'Angelo's for supper."

"You can't do that," said Marguerite.

"Why not?"

"You just can't. That's all."

Blue crossed her arms and crunched them into her chest. She put on her adorable anger act.

"If you don't let me do it, I'll run away. I'll sneak off when you don't know it and start over again like Momma did and leave you all alone with nobody to boss. You'll never find me, I swear it, cross my heart."

Marguerite felt the dangers falling out of the air again, thumping onto the sand around her, writhing in and out of her toes, twining up her legs. The danger of being alone forever crawled up her bony chest and wrapped itself around her neck.

"You must never do that!" The words hissed out of her closed throat on a thin stream of air.

"I'm going to do my plan, then."

Marguerite felt the pressure of Blue's arms around her waist and the glancing pull of Blue's fine, sticky hair across her shoulder.

"I would never really leave you," said Blue, and she bounced off toward the water like a kite in an unpredictable wind.

Between buses, Marguerite kept a sharp eye on Blue who had collected $2.75 by the time the flat, gray clouds rolled across the lowering sun and sent most of the families home for dinner. The mothers had given her quarters instead of dimes and the little ones she had watched over had hated to see their Mommas come back out of the ocean. Blue was so charming you could learn to love her in two seconds flat.

Marguerite had watched five buses arrive, let off their loads and lumber away, roaring over the road that led to town. The passengers got off carrying beach blankets and pails, wearing bathing suits and sandals. None of them wore heart shaped sunglasses with red frames and a black T-shirt that said "Foxy" in sparkly letters. None of them had carried a reluctant recognition for her in their eyes underneath the dark of the glasses. The last two buses, more people got on than got off.

The rain that came about seven in the evening sent everyone rushing with shirts and blankets over their heads to the edge of the beach to wait for the bus to take them home. The man who had lifted Blue out of the water was carrying his own daughter, sheltering her head from the rain, just like Momma had done the time they got caught in the storm walking home from seeing "Bambi," trying to save bus money. That was so long ago, before Blue, when it was only Momma and Marguerite, the happy, comfortable two of them in that long, cold soaking rainstorm that didn't matter a bit inside of Momma's thin, soft arms.

Marguerite and Blue pulled the hoods of their sweatshirts up over their heads when the first big drops skidded into the sand. Marguerite expected Blue to start complaining about being hungry and tired and wet, but instead, Blue offered her a piece of bubble gum and chomped on one herself. Between the two of them, there was only the juicy spit-cracking of the gum and the thudding of the rain.

Marguerite interrupted the sounds with words.

"Where'd you get the gum?"

"Mrs. Ferguson, the lady with the twins. She gave it to me with my quarter."

"You didn't beg it, did you?"

"I *saved* it till now. Just like you would. Aren't I smart to save it?" Blue twirled her hair. "Just like you, Ems."

Marguerite suddenly couldn't bear the idea that Blue might be white and beautiful and charming and smart, all at the same time.

"You begged it, I know you did." Marguerite knew she was saying it out of pure spite, but she couldn't help herself.

"No, honest. I didn't." Blue sounded indignant.

"You begged it. Nothing will make me think different," Marguerite insisted.

"I didn't. I didn't!" Blue began thudding her soft knuckles into Marguerite's arm. The bone buzzed and ached.

Marguerite grabbed Blue's shoulders and shook her.

"You did, you little snake. You tell me the truth," Marguerite shouted. "You just go off and do what you want to, no matter what I tell you. You just go off like that and leave me!"

Blue's face was shaking and chattering in front of her like an old movie. No, it was saying, no, no, no.

Marguerite flung it away and started stomping the sand, hitting and twirling, watching the beach and Blue and the bus stop and Mr. D'Angelo's whirl by and by and by until all of her thumped crazily onto the quilt. She collected her arms and legs into herself and sat there.

Blue brought her face in close and talked in slow motion. "We got to go, Ems."

"She told us to wait," Marguerite said before she had to close her throat down against the heavings that rose inside and dissolved against the barrier. She built a careful fence around her brain, and thought of nothing and nothing and nothing again.

Blue stood up and forced her jelly shoes on over her squeaky, wet feet. She bent down again and Marguerite felt each sneaker grate over her sandy, brittle toes and snap up over her heel.

"I have a plan," said Blue. "Let me do my plan."

Marguerite meant her voice to be definite, but it whispered itself and flew away on the wind like a boat whistle in the night.

"When Momma's gone, I'm the Momma."

Marguerite felt Blue roll her off the bed quilt. She watched Blue bunch up the material and hike it under her arm. She felt Blue's hand slip into her own and pull her to a stand.

"And when Momma's gone forever," said Blue, "we're just sisters again."

When Blue said that, the fence broke down in Marguerite's brain and the barrier she had set up against the retching gave way. Her throat was moving in horrible rhythm, and Blue was keeping time to it with her words, "It's okay, it's okay," and with her feet which were moving them slowly toward the house at the edge of the beach.

Marguerite's throat quieted for a while. Some words, bumpy and irregular, raw and thin, rose and escaped.

"I been keeping something," said Marguerite to her sister. "Momma gave it to us before she left."

"What is it?" asked Blue.

Marguerite drew a thin, rumpled twenty dollar bill from her sweatshirt pocket and held it out in front of them. It snapped and flew in the storm wind of the evening beach like a tiny ship's flag on a ten thousand mile sea.

Canyon Sam

♦

People Like This

I DODGE THROUGH a snarl of traffic over shards of broken glass to arrive at the neighborhood post office. There are only a few people in line—pensioners in mismatched clothes, young Latin women with bouncing children, working men in denim jackets, gum-snapping Filipino teenagers—a short wait for this busy substation near my home. I move quickly through the line and when a space opens at the far right counter, I take two giant steps and stand before her.

Her head is shaped like a crookneck squash with pale lips penciled in at the very bottom. Her cheeks have more brown specks than a grocery bin of russet potatoes. Wire-rimmed glasses cling firmly to the steep slant of her tiny nose.

Her eyes laser to the counter, cut a 135-degree angle along its surface and zero in on the unsealed envelope in my hand, like a bank shot into a corner pocket.

"I'd like sixty regular stamps. What's your latest issue?"

She tears out some green and yellow stamps from a shelf—a page and one row to make sixty.

"You can't send *that* that way," she remarks, indicating my envelope.

I look at the bulging envelope in my hands stuffed with a small film cartridge.

"It'll ruin fifteen other letters and shut down the whole machine."

"What?" I thought we were talking about stamps.

"Get one of those padded envelopes," she orders. "We don't have that small size. Mission Stationery between 23rd and 24th."

"I've sent it like this before many times," I protest. I have processed film through the mail in the past.

"It'll ruin fifteen other pieces of mail; it'll shut down the whole machine." She walks to the next cubbyhole and returns with a plastic guide. She takes my envelope between two fingers and dangles it like a fresh-caught minnow next to the black lines. The envelope is twice as wide as the marking.

"See, it's too big...Padded envelope...Mission Stationery between 23rd and 24th," she repeats.

"I *have* to have that?"

"Yes," she says coolly. "And money..." her eyes X-ray inside my envelope again. Wagging her head like a boy standing over a naughty puppy, she admonishes, "*Never* send cash. Never send cash. Never send cash through the maaay-yaal," whining the last word with weary intolerance.

"It's only a dollar."

The young Chicano next in line shifts his weight over his leather boots and scans the horizon of tellers. A buck, for Christ's sake.

"You can't send it like that; it has to be check or money order."

"How much are the stamps?" I ask, steering back. This is actually a simple transaction, I know it.

"Thirteen twenty," she snaps, almost without moving her lips, like a ventriloquist.

I open my checkbook, and on finding myself without a writing utensil, ask for one to use. She tilts the thin "U.S. Government" pen between her fingers toward me. "Next time, bring your own." I'm not sure I'm hearing right. I stop writing and raise my head to look at her. "There will be times when you and I both need to use it at the same time," she rejoins. They must not have the verb "share" in her language.

"We used to have them here," she notes with a quick contemptuous glance at the nubs that looked like they once held pens on the customer's side of the counter. "And *there*. . ." she stabs another glare in the direction of the waiting area behind me, ". . .on all the counters." I can almost see smoke snaking out from behind her Ben Franklin glasses, like the white stinging vapor that comes off dry ice.

"People ripped them right out," she says with a sideways tone like: 'It's you and your type of mixed-up, crime-ridden, bad-taste dark people and your common thievery that have forced the discontinuance of free pen use for the general public at this post office.'

"Who do I make this out to?"

"San Francisco Postmaster. . .You make it out to the postmaster of the city you're in. . . If you're in San Rafael, you write it to the San Rafael Postmaster. . .If you're in Pacifica, it's the Pacifica Postmaster." She is like Miss Nancy on Romper Room gone awry. Still instructive, still patronizing, but oh-so-sour.

I hand her my check and lay out my identification: a driver's license and a bank guarantee card.

"Driver's license, major credit card," she drills. My bank card is from a neighborhood savings and loan a few blocks away. "Huh-uh," she wags her head. "We don't take these guarantee cards."

"One has to qualify to get these cards. You have to go through a credit check and keep a minimum balance," I plead. I am not about to leave without the simple thing I came for.

"They're not on our system." The loose brown curls jostle back and forth as she shakes her head and pinches her pale lips together in a line.

"I've made out checks here before and it's always been okay,' . assert.

She strains to read the small print of the plastic bank card.

"It's all I have—the only other thing I have is a Blue Cross card or AAA. I live a block away, I come here all the time. And I always pay by check. I've got a few hundred dollars in this account right now."

"But this doesn't meet our requirement. We need a major credit card."

I flip through my checkbook for listings of past purchases from this very office. "Look," I point, reading down the lines, "March 3rd, Postmaster, $21.88...May 17th, Postmaster..."

"It doesn't matter. You don't have anything that will cover this check."

"It's going to cover *itself!*" I stare at her. I feel my feet become roots of a tree sinking a hole into the floor. Indignation courses through them, dropping the roots down, spreading them wide; my slow rage at her implications cements them into the marble floor

"You see," she says, scrutinizing my check with her band saw eyes. "If I okayed this, I'd have to put my own paycheck on the line If I initial this check and it goes through and doesn't clear, the amount would be taken from *my* salary!"

I stand squarely in front of the teller space. Not budging.

Faced with my resoluteness, she turns and walks out of my view . can hear her complaining to someone in the back: ". . . blah blah blah blah credit card...blah blah blah blah paycheck.. ."

Minutes later, she emerges with a large black woman in a knit business dress. The set of this middle-aged civil servant's face bemoans job pressure, overwork, steady nerves, and insane boredom. This woman doesn't so much as wink half an eyebrow at me; she follows the clerk to the counter, scribbles her approval, and walks back through the door without missing a beat.

"Ordinarily, we couldn't *take* your check," Miss Nancy scolds with a tone like: 'These are hardball rules, kid.' "But my boss put *her* paycheck up against it."

This lady could incite peaceful people to riot. I zip my belongings into my floppy backpack to leave. In all of this madness I almost forgot my reason for coming. I look around for the stamps; they are nowhere in sight.

With deft efficiency, she turns from the waist and lifts them up off a table behind her. Save Grassland Habitats. Pictures of ground squirrels and gophers coming out of wheat and grass and other bright spring colors.

At some point when I wasn't looking she had whisked the stamps off the counter, safely out of my reach. I fold up the one page and one row of peaceful benevolent gophers and grasshogs. Somebody at the post office has some humaneness, but it isn't at this desk. I steal away from her counter without a word.

"Thank you," I hear her clip to my departing back as I thread my way around the line of customers. As if for a moment she thought we could speak the same language.

Patricia Roth Schwartz

◆

Sunspots

I T'S LABOR DAY in Connecticut, steamy as a chestnut on Fifth Avenue in winter. My mother's making Christmas ornaments, wants me to help. This involves sitting at the dinette table, usually cluttered with piles of newspapers ("I just caint," she laments through the faint traces of her Applachian accent, "throw anything away."), poking slivers of steel through the very eyes of iridescent sequins, then sinking the pins deep into the hearts of styrofoam balls. Each year for the garden club boutique she produces five hundred of these wondrous objects, five hundred less than the number of plastic bags that live inside her bread drawer.

"Ma," I say, "can't we do something else?" My mood, low enough since I've been hanging around since Thursday, has not been improved by the appearance yesterday of my sibling, Sharon. As usual, she's got her fiance, David, in tow. This visit's purely duty for them, not to mention a pit stop on the way up north. In fact, they're outfitting themselves right now to canoe the Allagash, no easy task since they're not only all-natural but gourmet.

At thirty, Sharon's four years my junior. She's an editor for a

New York publishing firm. David's a tenured professor of economics at N.Y.U. They plan to get married as soon as they can decide whether to trek in Nepal or scale the Andes for their honeymoon. I teach English as a Second Language in a cold church basement funded by a grant that probably ran out last Tuesday. My latest lover's left me: in a good year, I average three; in a lean one there's nobody to lose.

Sharon and David just drove off in their Audi to purchase little backpack envelopes of freeze-dried stroganoff. Ma senses my restlessness. Anxious to please, lest I take off on her, too, she offers, "We could go out back." As we make our way out, she lights up another filter-free Camel. Ma's smoked for sixty years, ever since she and her brothers used to sneak out back the shed and smoke catalpa pods. You couldn't get a high from them, she's told me, but it was wicked all the same.

The air, now, in this large suburban split-level ranch in which the windows are never opened, reeks of nicotine; every room's cluttered with the excreta of my mother's life as it's evolved over the years. Starting out as typist in Columbus, Ohio, as far as she could get from West Virginia, Ma met my father, the son of a revenuer from the North Carolina backwoods. He'd gone from the pickle factory, during the depression, to accountant trainee in a mattress company, to sales director forty years later. She came to be able to afford excess: the plastic bags, the sequins, the styrofoam balls, green felt Christmas trees, yarn octopi with pigtail legs, old handbags limp with fatigue, tangled clumps of costume jewelry. Now, she could no more let any of it go than drown one of us.

"I need to water the amaryllis." Ma nudges me down the back steps. We end up on the patio where a redwood picnic table on unbalanced legs lists under its burden: shards of clay pots, a spider plant and all her progeny, one huge fern, and, below, rusted, empty window boxes, plastic plant flats, a dented bucket, garden tools, and some items whose identities remain obscure. It looks like

Egypt, Maine. I can't help imagining I can see, out of the corner of my eye, the wheelless carcass of an abandoned Chevy. But no, nothing's there save the astroturf lawns and turquoise pools of the neighbors; both have erected gigantic fences so Ma's picnic table can't be seen as they lunge, of a weekend, into chlorine.

"I haven't spoken to Elsie Zipko in three years," Ma gestures to the right with her cigarette, "not since Pierre died." She's dripping ash onto her floral cotton housecoat; three large burns already decorate its surface. Pierre was Elsie's poodle; Elsie left him all day to work in a bank as a data processor. While she was gone, he made a noise like a squeeze toy ten hours a day nonstop. When cancer was discovered it was too late. We'd assumed his pain came only from loneliness. Perhaps, after all, it had. "And Phyllis," that's the neighbor to the left, "I haven't talked to her in four years. Last time was the day of the hurricane. I saw her during the eye."

Now Ma's watering her amaryllis. There are twelve of them, lined up on the picnic table's benches which border the cracking flagstone patio: one for every Christmas my parents have had the house. The instructions say with careful watering and feeding a new set of blooms will appear a second year. None of my mother's have. Each stands now mute: no trumpet-shaped blooms, tall fronds drooping from each withered bulb. Still, she waters, tends, hopes.

"Where's Daddy?" I ask. I'm stinking with sweat, polo shirt sticking to my nipples, throat raspy with humidity and cigarette smoke. I'd like to tell Ma about my latest romantic failure, but I know from past experience all I'll get are reproaches, and lectures on things like shaving my underarms. Then, later, she'll tell me how she stays up late, listening to Sally Jesse Raphael, the shrink who talks on the radio, all about "love problems," and crying for me.

"He's at the short-wave." Ma shuffles over to the faucet on the side of the house, fills her watering can.

I'm not surprised. My father converses fluently in four languages, learned initially in night school, improved on later in the service, with people all over the world on the short-wave radio rig he installed awhile back. I say people: really, they're men (few women have leisure and money for amateur radio status; usually they're C.B.'ers with cute "handles" like "Doll-Baby" or "Powder Puff.") Daddy talks to men all over the place: Albuquerque, Rio, Cleveland, West Berlin. His favorite, though, comes from Marseilles. Georges, a civil servant who lives with his aging parents and his pet squirrel, used to call Daddy every morning, up until this year when sunspots intervened, rendering transmission impossible. Georges still writes, though, on whisper-thin transatlantic paper, and sends him books like *Captain Fracas*, a kind of French wild west sheriff.

In fact, I can hear right now, faintly, through the open basement-level window, the hum of the radio, the occasional crackle of energy along the high-tension wires that link these men, land to land, each spilling out to another what secrets they dare. As far as I can tell, the talk is always about how big of a rig they have, how much power it can handle. Men everywhere are really the same, always talking about their equipment. Daddy seems out of sync, somehow; he's looking for foreign language speakers, other displaced persons.

Once Daddy talked to me, the week his father died. He spoke with his eyes turned resolutely away from my face, told me all about how the kids up north where his family finally moved used to make him the butt of persecution, laughing at his backwoods accent. I guess that's why I keep hanging around—hoping to catch some more of the story.

The other thing Daddy has is telephones, a little odd, really, since he hasn't got any friends to talk to, unless you count Mario, the barber, or Morris across the street. The phones he got mostly at tag sales, some by mail from *Popular Mechanics*. They've all got special features, like digital calendars, or the capacity to store frequently-used numbers for push button recall. Daddy's got four numbers stored: me, Sharon, Mario, Morris.

One Christmas, hoping to capitalize on this newest fad, I got him a digital watch, and even a digital ball point pen: it told the date in teeny numerals along the barrel. I thought the pen would go nicely with the clock Daddy got from "the girls" in his office when he retired: the clock splays the lighted time across the ceiling while you lie in bed at night, the numerals changing second by second. But he never liked those things as well as the phones. One of them's cordless. When my mother carried it out one day while watering the amaryllis, it rang. Overjoyed (no one calls her either, except the garden club chairwoman asking for styrofoam balls), she told the person at the other end, a wrong number, how nice it was he'd called her in the garden.

Daddy's got another phone now, a touch-tone, hooked up to a place that tells you the stock market reports when you push the buttons. The electronic pulses sound like Close Encounters. The voice that tells you what your stock is doing, or not doing, is that of a computer. It (she?) is female—assuming, of course, that gender for computers, is a valid concept. Sometimes, like when another lover has left, I'd like to call her up. It would be a voice, after all. I can't reach Georges and don't know how to find the wrong number in the garden.

After another cigarette, my mother shuffles into the house again, insisting on my presence, to watch her 1:00 p.m. show. It's on every day, and seems to feature a nun who's frequently pregnant. Then, I have to make a sandwich for myself and for Daddy or we won't get lunch. We usually have deviled ham on whole wheat Home Pride. This last's a concession to Sharon and David who only eat whole, live foods. (I wonder if freeze-dried stroganoff was once whole?) With deviled ham, we always have a smattering of pickle relish, the green kind. During a commercial my mother supervises the amount of spread I'm allowed to put on each slice of bread.

"No, no, Debbie, that's too much. No, don't use that knife." Her brow knitted with anxiety, she whips one knife out of my hand, rummages in a drawer of utensils worthy of a medieval enforcer's collection, and hands me another which appears identical. I take it without rebuttal; having no Audi to escape in, I've long since learned how to survive on site.

Next, I take the sandwiches on a tray downstairs to my father. Since the upper regions of the house are hers—monopolized by the plastic bags, the octopi, the rejected jewelry, not to mention the India print bedspreads she's got all over the "good furniture" in the living room—he's had to carve out such territory as he could. The lower reaches work out fine: for one thing, they're cooler; for another, with her shuffling walk (which she claims just started a few months ago, at about the time her handwriting shrank several centimeters in size), it's hard for her to negotiate the stairs.

He's got it made down there, really. There's a large room we call the recreation room, complete with an ancient leather-padded bar behind which he keeps various lethal liqueurs—the artichoke for example, could take the rust right off your lawn furniture—some of which hide in a secret cubbyhole behind a trick panel. Here, also, Daddy positions his radio and several of his phones. A huge chess set, procured at a tag sale, dominates the rest of the room. It's the size of a bridge table with pieces about the height of ketchup bottles. He's never forgiven me for only learning how the pieces move, no strategy. Therefore, I can't play. It's been a problem I've had most of my life. Still, I remember my grandfather, before his death, visiting, sitting up night after night over that board with Daddy, never winning, just setting up those knights and bishops one more time. Not me, boy. David won't play either, even though he knows how. He always asks, instead, for bridge, at which he's an ace, never Trivial Pursuit. He knows I can beat him: he's desperately weak on early TV.

"David giggles," Daddy says, the only reason he'll ever give for hating the guy. Me, I've got lots more; David's fond of telling me how he makes fifty thousand dollars a year teaching two courses while I make a mere fifteen thousand. "Yeah, but," I always throw back, "I don't have to hang out at faculty meetings." David never answers, just slinks off to the guest room where they keep their gorp in zip-lock plastic bags. I do think plastic is a dead substance; I wonder if they know.

"David giggles; he's not a man's man," Daddy repeats himself. Presumably, though, Georges is, and also Morris, who once, in his cups, a frequent occurrence, backed his car down his own driveway, across the street, and up my parent's sloping lawn to leave tread marks on the slim trunk of a young maple my mother had been growing from its own wings these past six years.

Mario, the barber, is not a man's man either. Desperately fond of my father (that dog-like devotion makes sense to me: it's what's driven every one of my lovers away), he likes to call him in the evenings to speak Italian, sends him books on Tuscan architecture and the opera, gives him special bottles of wine after every haircut, plus stamps he's soaked off letters from his sister still over in Naples. My father despises these offerings, makes fun of them, considers letting his hair grow out. Nevertheless, every Thursday he returns for a trim, even offered to call Mario's sister on the short-wave through a phone patch to Naples. Creatures of habit and need, my parents. Standing in the garden, I wonder for a fleeting instant if the amaryllis ought to be moved more into the sun?

Sharon and David return from their shopping trip to Eddie Bauer where a marathon Labor Day sale was taking place. Daddy and I call it Eddie Bow-Wow: in the absence of real conversation, we indulge in puns, wordplays, double entendres (never sexual, of course), anything the others can't catch onto, especially Ma. It gives me a sense of solidarity I get nowhere else, except, perhaps, on the first days of terms when my students, terrified Cambodians and Haitians, gather with me to begin to learn how to survive in an alien land. Besides, it beats the hell out of getting checkmated.

"Look what we've got!" Sharon's pulling packages out of the Audi, talking nonstop. Thin, sharp-featured, relentlessly perky, she manages to pour forth an uninterrupted conversational stream throughout entire visits. This seems to function as a kind of Star Wars energy shield. I guess she feels she needs it. After all, no one in the family likes David, she's not my parents' favorite, won't make puns or sequined balls, thinks artichoke liqueur gives you cancer, and amaryllis only need watering once a week. She seems to believe that chattering away about the books on her publishing list can prevent David and Daddy from locking horns like stags on Wild Kingdom, or me snuffling on about romance down the tubes.

"Your standards are too high," she tells me brightly each time I flounder again. Now, looking at David, as he rummages through the Eddie Bauer bags to show us his many-pocketed vest, his fanny pack, his cans of sterno, I'm glad. I see Sharon wince now every time David hears Ma say, "I reckon." I feel sorry for her embarrassment, remember how close we once were, playing Ginny dolls and dyeing our mashed potatoes blue. I'd try to talk to her more now if she didn't keep recommending I get a better haircut.

She's going on now about one of her authors, the doctor whose book, *How to Live as Long as Possible*, explains every imaginable way one might eat, exercise, sleep, excrete, think, and have sex to achieve extraordinary longevity. Whether a particular individual wants to, or even ought to, live that long is not discussed. Sharon and David are suitably impressed by the good doctor, plan to follow his regimes to the letter. Sharon's only worry is that the guy has the personality of a used Brillo pad, can't be considered for talk shows, and therefore the book won't be a best-seller. She's never had one: the Children's Bible in twelve volumes sold in supermarkets just didn't make it, nor did the cards on house plants tucked adorably into a plastic greenhouse file (my mother got one free; she keeps earrings without mates in it and opened and unopened bags of sequins).

"Here comes Morris," my mother says. We're all standing in the driveway, the Eddie Bauer bags perched on the hood of the car. Myself, I travel by bus. "Be nice to him. Ever since his mother died, he's very unhappy." I can still see the tread marks on the maple, and I know. "After she died, Meals on Wheels forgot to cancel her order. He gets two meals every time, and tries to bring them over here. Daddy likes them, but I don't."

"They use white bread," Sharon sniffs, "and canned vegetables. That's an appalling diet for senior citizens. Dr. Brewer says—"

"Morris was a staff sergeant in the U.S. Army," Daddy interrupts, threateningly, as if daring David to giggle. "He was in the offensive up Omaha beach." Daddy, who was a communications officer in the Allied invasion of Italy, never talked war stories until David came into the picture. Sharon and I, mere females, couldn't be trusted to grasp it all. Somehow David's testosterone qualifies him. Daddy's favorite (which David always listens to silently from behind his wire-rims, before he slips off for a date-fig-apricot chew) is about how he had to stand in front of a four-star general and explain why his jeep had gotten stolen by Fascisti. This was somewhere outside Bologna in 1944.

"I told him the truth," Daddy reminds us for the thousandth time. "Always tell the truth. It saves on complications. I told him, 'I left the keys in it.' "

"Let's hear about Omaha beach, Sergeant," Daddy hails Morris heartily, as our neighbor shuffles up the drive, honing in, like radar, on the source of human noise we represent. I wonder idly where the cordless phone is, could we hear it ringing, for example, if it were stuffed under a sofa cushion, or smothered by plastic bags?

"Omaha Beach...Yes, sir," Morris starts out in a peppy tone, which sinks rapidly. "That was when I got the letter telling me Dad was failing." He searches each one of us, face by face. Behind us, through the open garage door, from the depths of the recreation room, I hear the crackle and whine of the radio. Perhaps Georges is calling. With the sunspots due to leave pretty soon, now he and Daddy should have another eleven years, free and clear, until the cycle comes round again. "That was very hard on me." Morris beseeches each one of us mutely in turn. "I flew right home, but when I got there they'd put him in the ground."

Tight-lipped, my mother moves closer to him. Within her (I know, from every crisis I've ever had, the few I've ever let her know about, anyway) war wages between the horror of emotional mess, personal dishonor, and the yearning her own pain has for company. "That was very hard for you, Morris," she murmurs, her accent slurring the words. She grubs in the pocket of her house coat for another Camel.

"I told him," Daddy says louder, " 'I left the keys in it.' Always tell the truth." I'm shifting, now, from foot to foot, wishing I were home in Boston. My old bedroom here, where I sleep now, has in it the clock that flashes the time all night on the ceiling. I just can't take it. I miss my tiny apartment, neat and spare as a military barracks. I miss my two cats, Watson and Holmes, and their antics. I miss my students, their gratitude, their surprising senses of humor, the walks we take after their lessons are done, practicing with street signs and using American money. There's no one here to play with, unless I want chess. I know how to open the secret wine compartment. Even Pierre is gone.

"We're going for a walk, Ma," Sharon announces. David's moved closer to her side. His spindly, hairy legs hang down from his khaki, canvas, many-pocketed shorts. He takes her hand. "Honey, let's do three miles. We've got to get in better shape for Mount Katahdin."

"Mother's gone now, too, you know," Morris tells us, ignoring everything else. His eyes close up look rheumy, pale, naked blue. "I go out alone," he says. "I talk to myself alone."

Morris, I look at him, I understand.

Jennifer Krebs

◆

Isn't This How Rituals Begin?

R ELATIONSHIPS. SOME PEOPLE say from the first moment
you can tell where they'll lead. Heightened expectations
from a chance meeting, an inflection of the voice, the curl of a
fingertip around a crystal glass at an elegant party. Working
together on the planning committee of an event of major
proportions, like a Take Back the Night march. Only you see eye-
to-eye on issue after issue and you will not be separated ever after.

Other people say relationships are clarified in the ending. The
ultimate exposure of all the faults, crevices, rotten habits, and
pitiful ideas. So that if you're ever at the same party or Take Back
the Night march, you wait and watch from so far away that you
remain a shadow, a dream, a breath of the past.

I don't believe in any of this. It's like how you go about writing
history. After the fact, it's easy to say the water was green and the
air blue. You can ignore the hues and make a clear point. Maybe
that helps you get on with your life. As for me, some of my best
relationships got off to rotten starts and I've never parted ways with
a lover over bad habits or lack of love. No, one or maybe both of

us lacks a conviction to proceed. We retreat, like after a rainfall on a hot hot day, when the water thickly, steamily evaporates almost as soon as it stops falling. And so to see each other again is not a curse but part of an inescapable cycle.

Where this leaves me is with the guts, the day-to-day, the insides of the relationship. How you live your life. Right? How it is happening. Where the changes come, and where they don't. Because where there's change there's a future.

I didn't invent any of this myself. My friend Libby and I talk about this stuff. And I can vouch, using our own relationship as an example, that these theories work.

Libby and I have known each other a long time. First we were pals. We'd have lunch, a movie, bowl, theorize, plot revolution—pretty easy stuff. Then after this particular interaction...

It was Christmas eve and raining. And, in spite of the fact that I was twenty-eight years old, and had been menstruating more or less monthly for fifteen years, I had not a tampon or a pad in the house. Ho ho ho. Safeway, I found out after a bunch of phone calls, was the only place open. (It was not my first choice.)

As the sliding doors of the Safeway opened to let me in, I told myself I would not participate. I repeated a litany under my breath—*get the tampons, get the Advil, get to the check out and get out*—as I walked down the aisle.

Damn, but I slid on some tinsel into the wall of sanitary napkins.

"Beth," I heard a voice. "Watch what you're doing!" It sounded like my mother. My mother? She doesn't live around here. I looked up.

"Libby?"

I would have picked myself up then, I think, but the p.a. system came on: "Shoppers, Safeway will close in ten minutes." I froze staring off at the napkins.

Libby noticed my glazed look. "What is it?" she asked.

"Advil," I said hesitantly, "I've got to get to it. Get it. Get to the check out. Get."

"Well then, Beth," she said, "Get up. I'll get the Advil and meet you at the check out."

"No, don't leave me. I'll never get out of here. I'll turn into the ghost of Christmas present."

"Okay, Beth." She looked at me firmly. "Give me a box of those pads." (I gave her a box.) "Get up." (I got up.) "Hold onto the back of this wheelchair." (I grabbed the handles.) Libby turned on the juice so fast I practically fell again.

We were out of there in no time. I perked up once I hit the cold rain outside. "My hero," I said to Libby.

A simple ending, no?

No. If it was simple there would have been no change.

I said, "Libby, I want to take you home and tuck you into bed. You really saved me just now."

She said, "But no, you need pampering. I'll go home with you and see that you take your Advil and relax."

"But no!" I said emphatically, "Please let me thank you, let me show my appreciation. My hero."

"Hero, shmero."

After several more quips, I noted that we were wet and I was getting clammy. I heard my mother's voice: Only clams can be clammy and not get sick. "Libby," I said, "We've got to stop this."

She said, "I see a compromise." (She really is a great person to work on a Take Back the Night march with, she always has these compromises.) "The compromise is this. Tonight I let you take me home and tuck me in. But next month we rendezvous here. Same thing. And I come to your house and tuck you in."

. . . Isn't this how rituals begin? And isn't ritual a foundation for living?

For a number of years, Libby and I celebrated this monthly

ritual. Called each other friends, not pals. Devised theories of relationships, planned our futures. Calculated the amount of risk involved in telling the truth in various situations and the amount of hope involved in not telling the truth but implying it.

Then I moved to the California Coast north of San Francisco, a small town called Point Reyes. Libby still lived in Berkeley just two blocks from the Safeway. It wasn't like we changed back from friends to pals, there was still a connection beyond bowling and movies and plotting the overthrow of tyranny in its many forms. But you know how these long distance friendships are: long distance.

One Sunday morning I was sitting in the Blue Whale Cafe drinking some Earl Grey, looking out across Rte. 1 at Tomales Bay. I wasn't looking for whales. I was just looking the way I do when I'm off in a daydream. Looking more in than out. Kind of miraculous. When else can you see in so many directions than when you're daydreaming?

I'm thinking about this map I've seen. The earth fifty billion years from now. On this map the peninsula of Point Reyes is detached from California and up by the Aleutian Islands. The result of major earthquakes and continental drift. Having moved to Point Reyes, I see this map often. Not that I expect to live to fifty billion. But it keeps my senses in check. Tomales Bay so blue and hazy, with the many small boat docks, some of them floating, and the birds diving in for fish. In just a few earthquakes: Tomales Strait. Perhaps a bridge erected where now I sit, linking Reyes Isle with the Mainland. Only the blue water endures. Of course, if we humans continue to enjoy ourselves in toxic manners, perhaps the water will look orange reflecting a gold sky. Who knows?

I see myself in a black car driving off into an orange sky on a purple road. I accelerate. The sun sets through the gridded windows of the Blue Whale. I wonder where I'll be tomorrow. The door opens and Libby comes in.

"Libby? What are you doing here?"

She says, "Do you know that today is the day of the harmonic convergence? I'm going to the Point. Everything is going to change. Come with me."

Where is the melody to this harmony? I wonder as Libby and I drive out to the Point Reyes lighthouse. There is nothing to be seen but water. Not the water or sky of my daydream. Something more familiar, comforting. I can't say, in fact, that it looks different from yesterday: air water blue. The convergence of the water in its different forms.

Libby tells me that this event is major. Major not like Point Reyes is going to be changed from Peninsula to an Aleutian Island overnight like express mail. Or like Christmas, Safeway, or Advil. But major in that the whole world will never be the same again. That tomorrow will look different and feel different and be different.

"Amen, Libby, amen," I say. "I felt this way yesterday and today nothing new. I'm ready for change. Let's celebrate." So I jump up and down and she turns wheelies and we both scream and kiss. Libby says this is a good ending. With the heroes in high spirits and the sun above the water. I am less certain of this than I am about Point Reyes becoming an Aleutian Island. But since the world is changing, I'm willing to agree.

Katharine Haake

♦

All the Water
in the World

1

♦ ♦ ♦

I F YOU LOOK closely enough at any landscape, you will see
clearly how whatever is human in it is an overlay, an intrusion.
Some landscapes are closer to this raw fact than others. You think
that because I tell stories it is the human part that interests me, but
in fact I have always been fascinated by the convergence of things.
Our lives are played out, after all, on surfaces which, familiar,
reassure, but then from time to time we—all of us, really—run
across a situation where the elements are in disjunction, where
nothing quite fits.

This particular road comes in from above, and the path you take
down from it winds past the privy through an immature orchard
of what in the summer will yield golden apples and plums, maybe
pears, to the house, which, like the privy, is built of unwhitewashed
adobe, straw jutting out from where the mud has rubbed away,
with turquoise and emerald green trim. Outside there is clutter:
some milkcans, a chainsaw and tools, three washlines, cracked
pottery planters. To you, it will seem bleak, these low crude walls,

the gray day and its uninterrupted snow. It will seem, perhaps, alien, too. Is this another country? Can yucca really grow, as it appears, where January gets so cold and just below that stand of pines?

I am only giving facts, of which I am in full possession of all that could be called quite necessary. The river that flows through the floor of this valley—you can see it below, wide, spewing froth around rocks—diminishes in summer, bled almost dry, at times, by irrigation. That stand of pines you noticed, a little higher up, gives way to thick evergreen forest. Thus we have come to that exact spot where desert and alpine vegetation encroach on each other from below, from above. As a consequence, this dry earth is ripe for anything. Even now, if you stray from the path, though you may stumble in snow, burrs will snag at your clothing, and if a dog curled at the door of the house it would yelp wildly in—what, surprise or warning? But there isn't any dog.

Only the house itself, which is tiny: two small rooms opening out on one another through a crude split-log archway, and an adjoining greenhouse, rooms without logic, half window, half mud. One has high-tech track lighting; the others, no lighting at all. And though there is water tapped in from the well, it is hot (on demand) only in the claw-footed bathtub on the dirt floor of the greenhouse, which contains, in addition to the tub and a thriving winter garden, a mechanical swing for a baby and a slightly used Maytag washing machine. Imagine your bath in that tub, low down to the earth, weeds and crickets pressing up against the glass just at the level of your face, just where you reach for the soap. It is a luxury of fusion. In such a wealth of steam, you are eye-to-eye with snow. Similarly, in the next room what you will find are these: a woodburning cookstove (the sole source of heat) and a high narrow double bed; also, a kitchen sink, some plywood shelves, a stereo and chifforobe, a table, four chairs, and one small humpbacked refrigerator, the kind that, like clockwork every three months, the cold storage compartment, barely big enough for ice cream, freezes solid and has to be thawed. Between this room and the greenhouse, in the other proper room, on an old blue steamer chest, an early model Kaypro computer shows the text of what appears to be a poem. One wall is lined with shelves that hold canned goods and books. Two corners are partitioned off with Navajo blankets behind which are hidden a small army cot and a crib.

In this way, out of the piling on of detail, a sense of the lives played out upon this piece of land, twelve acres in all, begins to emerge, but it deceives: I have, for instance, proof that the people who have settled here hold Ph.D's and responsible positions in the town twenty miles to the west. Their baby, delivered at home, was covered by Blue Cross. They own a red Toyota truck and are fond of Big Macs and beer. Though it may seem helter-skelter, what they've done here, it is in fact clearly designed. Give Chuck a drink or two and he'll hold forth with eloquence on each of what will be the next three rooms, the corral, the two gentle horses, and the son who will tend them. Even Bitsy, more circumspect by nature and increasingly shy, will talk enthusiastically about a separate kitchen with hot water and, maybe someday down the road, irrigation for her garden, a bedroom for the girl. Or they would have once, a long time ago it seems, back at the height of the Indian summer when the sky was hard and blue enough to shatter, you could almost believe, like an ancient piece of clay and the earth it spread over seemed almost to shimmer, part red, part gold—before, in other words, the day they put the cot up and Bitsy's crippled mother came to stay.

2
◆ ◆ ◆

When Bitsy was born, her mother examined each minute part

of her body and pronounced her, for all practical purposes, perfect. She had such high hopes for the child. Now, more than thirty years later, Bitsy endured, as she had every day for three months, the same anxious scrutiny, the same unrelenting assessment. Thus, though ordinarily she would have been grateful for the snow which seemed, in this hard landscape, to mute things, easing the sharpness out of contours and softening packed surfaces, she had grown this late in the afternoon quite edgy and as close as she can let herself come these days to tears.

Chuck was outside splitting kindling. Bitsy could hear him. As she listened, she remembered the Indian summer, lying high in that bed with the tiny Clara at her breast, and the sensation of everything hovering just on the precipice of change, while outside Chuck methodically stacked firewood. It was like Clara's fists. For weeks, months even, she never once uncurled them; then all at once she was reaching for things, grasping them, letting them loose when she tired of them. Chuck hauled home truckload after truckload of wood, stockpiling it against a change of weather. Yet every day it was seventy degrees. Every day Bitsy took Clara down to the river to nurse in the heat of the afternoon sun. Now she tried to remember just when the weather changed. She tried to imagine the pleasure of impact, honed ax against mesquite. She longed for Clara to wake from her nap. And with a strength of will that surprised even her, she kept on refusing to turn to that corner of the room where her stiffbacked mother sat gripping the wheels of her wheelchair, watching her daughter, watching the snow.

"You should rouse her," June said. "I always roused you, and you slept through the night at seven weeks."

Bitsy shifted slightly, wetting her chapped lips with her tongue. "This air," she complained, "the fire dries it out so." Her face was composed, almost placid. If she could keep it that way until Chuck came in, they would make it to evening, cocktails, bed. And tomorrow, Bitsy told herself, no matter what, they would go into town to shop. They needed vegetables, milk. They were out of cheese. Chuck would want his whiskey. If they could make it: they weren't going to make it. Behind her, her mother was stirring, unlocking her chair, starting to work it toward Bitsy, rocking it back and forth across the uneven tiles, making clumsy progress, determined.

"What are you doing?" Bitsy heard herself ask.

"It's worse for the baby than for you. I'm putting water on the stove."

Let me help you, Bitsy knew she should say. She knew the sink was too high for her mother, the iron pot too heavy, the stove itself too much a source of her disdain. Only it was so still outside, so quiet, and the whiteness of it all. Even the high-reaching saguaro was capped with thick tufts of powder. Soon they would pass a record for continuous snowfall. *Let me help you*, Bitsy felt the words rise and then stop at her lips. *Don't strain yourself, Mother*. It was like a litany, while the world she discovered three years back continued to transform itself and she wanted nothing more than to go out into it, immersing herself in its unfamiliar coolness.

Bitsy had had this feeling before. She had it often when she and Chuck first came here, especially at this hour, though then it was summer and the afternoon bled late into the night. All day she would pack mud into the plywood molds Chuck had made, and then the light would catch a certain angle and Chuck would start on beer and the blue gama grass would glow an unearthly silver and Bitsy, half crazed with longing, would find herself wandering down, always down to the river, which trickled through the valley all summer like a memory and promise of life. Bitsy meant to cash in on that promise. She had meant to since the day she first met Chuck at a benefit poetry reading and he told her about sunflowers in August.

"You can, in that part of the country," he said, "follow sunflowers for five hundred miles, one thousand miles. An accident of nature," he described them, and ordered two more beers. "Who could have intended so many sunflowers?" By the time they were through with their beer that night, Chuck looked straight into Bitsy's eyes and assured her, "The sweetest, saddest land you can imagine."

Thus, she was unable to conceive it when after that summer of making mud bricks, after the summer of putting them up and the winter of no running water and kerosene lamps, not even, that winter, a privy, and the following winter of pregnancy nausea, her mother had written of her needs and plans. Bitsy and Chuck had argued for a month afterward, until Chuck finally said, "She's your mother, Bitsy, I respect that. But not more than a couple of weeks, I want you to promise. We left all that, remember. We pulled up stakes and started new."

In this way the day came when Chuck rose before dawn to drive the five hours to the airport and five hours back while Bitsy sat, as even now she sits, for hours with her baby and considered as if for the first time just how it would seem to her mother: from the complex, humid suburbs she was leaving, through various airports to the red Toyota truck and the last part of her journey straight and fast down the freeway along the Rio Grande, up the state highway around intricate curves past endless county junctions with forgotten destinations, to the unimproved dirt roads above the riverbed, the crossing, the final dry climb among cacti to their rough, half-constructed adobe, two rooms opening out on each other with a dirt-floored, all-purpose greenhouse attached and a new compost privy out back. When the baby fussed, Bitsy attended to her, but as if she were a stranger, delicate and alien. She had considered everything, she thought, but not how it would seem to her mother, not in the actual moment, the now. In her head she reversed the journey, back down to the Rio Grande and there, another country. The idea was soothing to her. *Reverse everything*, she thought. She thought about the other country.

What Bitsy really thought about was how, more than anything, she wanted not to think about her mother, her husband, the wheelchair in the back of the truck. What she wanted was that the day should be no different from any other. What she did was transform the whole problem to one of concentration. *Reverse*, she thought again, *everything*. Very gently she dislodged her daughter from one breast to the other. She breathed in a pattern, rhythmic, deliberate. And she stared, though as if without seeing, down past the flowering yucca, past her overripe garden, past Chuck's young cottonwoods to the thin silver strand of the river below, its poor rocky valley, an old trailer park, and the low serene opposite mountains she loved.

Four months later those same humble mountains were entirely obscured by snow, but Bitsy knew their shape so perfectly she could trace their whitened humps and curves exactly in her mind. Behind her, her mother was still struggling with the pot of water, but Bitsy heard her as if from a far greater distance than was possible in their tiny house. It's the snow, she thought, how quiet it makes things, and still. Even Clara slept without stirring; even Chuck was strangely silent at his woodpile, probably making neat stacks of kindling, probably putting off coming inside. Or was he merely resting, leaning contemplatively against the red handle of his second-hand ax? Bitsy imagined him there, snow dusting his eyebrows and lashes. She imagined his head half cocked to the murmuring universe, just, she thought, outside these panes of glass. What would it take, she wondered, to set him loping off like a coyote, out across the frozen fields, up into the mountains, away from their homestead, herself, their daughter, and June? The thought of the mountains set off a furtive fluttering, like the dark wingspan of an ungainly bird just at the moment of flight, in Bitsy's heart, and she steeled herself against the determined splashing behind her.

Twice already her mother had filled the pot, then found herself unable to lift it up out of the sink. Now she was cradling the pot in her lap and using a thick coffee mug to ladle water from the tap. Because the sink was full of dishes, either way it was awkward and difficult; and the water, this time of year, was always icy. June's fingers were puckered and white. Bitsy longed to straddle her bird, like a horse, and let it loft her. Almost she could feel the brush of snow against her hot cheeks, turning, as they rose, into the envelopment of clouds.

When Bitsy's mother overturned the pot as she attempted to place it on the stove, only the baby cried out at the hiss of the steam, the clatter of iron on tile. June set her lips in grim but vindicated silence. Bitsy felt herself being swept under by a surge of resignation as she got up to comfort Clara.

"You're wet," she said to her mother. "Put on something dry."

"Do you have any butter?" her mother said. "My hand is burned."

Bitsy returned with the baby carried high on her shoulder and peered at her mother's red hand. "We have lard, but it will only seal the heat in. Run cold water over it. That will soothe it."

But her mother insisted on lard and the hand continued to redden. Chuck noticed it right off when at last, near dusk, he finished his chores and came inside bringing wood and bad news.

"Jesus," he said, "that must smart." Then he turned to Bitsy and said, "It's getting warmer."

"Warmer? At sundown? Is that normal?"

"Maybe the cloud layer's dropping. Maybe a new front is blowing in." He pulled off his boots, his soaked socks. "If it gets any warmer, I'll have to move the goats."

"In all this snow?" June muttered. "You must be mad."

"In case the snow starts melting, Mama. Could you hold the baby while I put up supper?"

But even as Bitsy said it she found herself staring at her mother's hand, cradled like a wounded animal in her mother's lap, still another injury, she thought, another handicap. Her mother sighed, not quite petulantly, and reached her good hand for Clara. Bitsy saw it, white and trembling, but ignored it, turning instead to the refrigerator where, if she added stock and onions, there would be enough black bean soup for another night. Chuck was drawing water in the greenhouse for his bath. Bitsy wanted to join him there. Now that night was coming on, without any moon, that endless white expanse outside was blackening, like tar. Bitsy thought about sinking deep into the steaming water of Chuck's bath, intertwining their legs, and letting the world outside close tight around them. This alone, she believed, would give them strength enough to hold the world there, suspended exactly as it was, just outside the window, just this cold. For however long it took, they would hold it off, and then when it was over, she would heat the soup, they would eat.

Instead, Bitsy put the baby on her sheepskin mat and started chopping onions. *Would you excuse us*, she could just imagine saying, *please, mother, as we hold off the world?* The onions brought tears to her eyes. Or Chuck, and Bitsy sighed, if she gave him half a chance, would start it up again, biting at her neck, groping at her breasts, whispering in her ear: *The visit is over now, Bitsy, I've had it. Choose her or choose me, I mean it this time.*

Meanwhile, the baby had started to whimper while June, still wet, fastidiously picked burrs from the sweater Bitsy had tossed at her. Chuck, in the next room, was quietly splashing. Bitsy felt amazed at so much human activity in such a small space. The smallness of the space increased her sudden keen sense that their individual actions might somehow determine the external course of events. *Maybe we will make it after all*, she thought, but in her heart she knew her mother could never be made aware of the consequences of even so simple a thing as a snowmelt, much less the complex figurations by which she held the baby, she did not hold the baby, who by now was crying in earnest. Bitsy was convinced that if no move were taken to comfort the child, no move either could be taken against night's heat, the fragile snow, the rising river, but she herself held an onion in one hand and a paring knife in the other and felt helpless to intervene in this first action. *Take action, Chuck,* she thought. She thought *Mama, take care of my baby.* She was listening very hard for some sign that this crisis, too, would pass. But Clara, so new at life and anxious for it, knew nothing yet of patience, and as her wails increased in intensity and volume, Bitsy could not stop herself.

"Could someone take my baby? Please, someone take my baby."

3
♦ ♦ ♦

Between Bitsy and Chuck it was what people used to call a "whirlwind romance." They were both on the late side of thirty and had spent their wad of dreams, or so it seemed to them before they met that night of the poetry reading three years earlier. Then, disillusioned in love and despairing of the future, they were both a little bit clumsy at life, lacking common social skills and overeducated. They were further attractive only in the way of people who do their best to hide it, Bitsy spurning make-up and Chuck never bothering to match his clothes or change his childhood haircut. There was something sad and plain about them, but there was an energy too, like the underside of anger, as if they had never quite got over a feeling of generalized outrage at life's not being fair. It wasn't fair in grade school that some people had money (Chuck) and others not (Bitsy). The war in Vietnam had not been fair, nor any of its consequences either. Whoever they slept with, it never really turned out fair, with Bitsy twice having abortions and Chuck losing lover after lover because of an intensity of longing, more exactly than desire, they were, being human, unable to assuage. And most of all, it had never been fair that not for a single instant of their lives had they been able, or later willing, to count on the future, to fill it, in good faith, with children, their children, laughter, prosperity, peace.

Thus it was, if not natural, then inevitable that they should find each other at that benefit where half a dozen local poets had gathered at a bar cafe to protest the only way they knew the end of everything. Bitsy, Chuck noticed, knew a few of the poets and spoke to them intently during breaks. Chuck was wearing a red and black *No First Strike* T-shirt Bitsy would have given all the rest of her T-shirts combined to own. For the first half of the evening they were careful not to meet each other's eyes; during the second, having hastily grabbed seats as the fourth poet began to read, they found themselves at the same small round table, each privately pleased and anxious to break what, under normal circumstances, would have remained a rigid silence.

One poet read a poem about a girl who exchanged her unlovely face for a death mask, black, with white slashes for features. Now, the girl looked grim and prophetic and some men, especially visionaries, found her hopelessly attractive. But though she lent her long, straight limbs and slender body willingly to their embraces, for she herself felt lush and full of passion, not one of them was able to penetrate what seemed to them instead a strange serenity. Thus, when she conceived, her children were stillborn. The men, too, languished and suffered.

"That was me," Bitsy told Chuck in a whisper. "I made the mask and hung it on my wall. What I meant was that suffering diminishes you, whereas we, in our current condition, if we plan to survive, must assume new and larger proportions."

The poet went on to his next poem as Chuck considered what Bitsy had said, which he found, despite himself, both noble and abstract. In no time at all he had decided he essentially agreed and that what was wrong in his life was that he always went for women who were more like the poet than Bitsy. The problem was to convince her. This was when he thought about the sunflowers. He himself was a geologist, nothing eloquent about him, but if it was grandness she wanted he could offer her landscapes, the permanence of rocks. He liked the way she put it: *in our current condition, if we plan to survive.* There was nothing wrong, he thought as he offered her a beer and she accepted, with changing plans that late (or was it early all along?) in life.

In this way they succumbed, each separately, to the uneasy sensation of things slipping out from under that comes when two people who have been unlucky in their dreams meet and discover it was never the dreams themselves that were at fault but just the way they went about them. For as long as she could remember, regardless of the risks, Bitsy had ordained it as her destiny to take a stand against annihilation by bearing a new generation, revising the future, yet twice she had emptied her womb. While what Chuck wanted more than anything was just that things not be complex, so he became a geologist. "This whole intricate earth," he likes to explain even now, "was formed and keeps forming itself through a few basic forces. It sloughs itself off; it uplifts itself. You have your Grand Canyon, your Mt. St. Helens, your oceans." But however just or logical his reasoning, Chuck's science was bound to betray him, leading as it did over the years away from the simple life he craved to inane academic entrenchment. Drawn as Chuck was to the field, he couldn't get out of the classroom. "When I would have been happy," he'd sometimes get drunk and confide to his students, "with my own piece of bedrock and some goats." There was more to his dream—a river, red sandstone, children playing somewhere just out of sight—but Chuck was, in most situations, acutely self-conscious, and the way his students looked at him, as if, quite by accident, he'd revealed something shameful, prevented him ever from mentioning the wife who wore her hair in a pigtail down her back and who could coax a garden from the desert.

Bitsy cropped her hair and had another dream, closer really to a hope, and less precise. For Bitsy had a private history, one that in her childhood had kept her out of Girl Scouts and dance class and that later on, in adolescence, perpetuated an unnatural isolation. "I'm not afraid of you," she told the occasional boy who showed any interest. "I just want to be left alone." She said it in such a way that the boy would never suspect that long before she could understand the cause or consequences, her father gave his life up for his country in another country and her mother, as if she never heard that times had changed since other wars, took to her bed, made an invalid by grief. Bitsy remembers the exquisite pallor of her skin.

"It was like what they would call in infants 'failure to thrive,' " she told Chuck that first night when the poems were done. "The way it is in books, but from another century: she liked for me to place cool cloths upon her brow."

There are other things Bitsy remembers too—a pale green nylon lace bedjacket, the half-sour smell of wilted chrysanthemums, and the way the day the President was killed her mother drew her lips into a thin gray line, and then uttered these three words, "It's a judgment." "I was just a little girl, Chuck," Bitsy said. "My father was dead and my mother kept insisting she'd never walk again."

Chuck had a habit of rubbing his left earlobe between his thumb and second joint of his forefinger. He was doing it now as he thought about what consoling thing he might say to this woman whose legs he was just beginning to notice had a tendency to curl around whatever they touched—the leg of her chair, the opposite ankle and calf. Chuck was sincere in his desire to make Bitsy feel better, but his heart was more on what those same extravagant legs would do let loose in bed. He thought of the various parts of his body as eyes for the hooks of her knees. "Hook me," he wanted to say. Instead he said nothing. He was aware of being tested. His own mother, somber faced, athletic and as vigorous as a woman half her age, sent him checks at holidays, his birthday. He remembered her as always freshening her lipstick. The last time she saw him she told him she pitied him. She was not an issue in his life.

Thus, almost in spite of himself and without any particular forethought, Chuck began redefining the issues, beginning that night with Bitsy's legs. And although he was aware of endless complications, he believed that if he concentrated on the small and intimate details of each day, he might somehow circumvent that other danger. He worked without a plan but with such a concentrated zealousness that by the time Bitsy introduced him to her mother (who offered him sherry and said, "It's an odd thing, how, when she is born, you have such high hopes for your child. Everything is expectation then, and promise." She spoke clearly, incisively, but without expression. "Thirty-three years later," she went on, straightening the knitted afghan at her knees, "your daughter brings a young man home who wears his Levi's cuffed two inches at the hem. Those are Levi's, aren't they?" she said) it was too late for them: they were in love.

Or Chuck was anyway. Bitsy was so intent on the chance he might be offering there wasn't room for feeling much, not hope yet and certainly not doubt. It was as if she had been hiding out all her life in order to make herself ready for just this particular moment and any emotion at all might jeopardize everything.

"I tried to tell you, Chuck," she said when they had left her mother's house for a nearby cafe, "and I mean what I say. You watch your mother fade like that, and what the hell, it's complicated. I'll do anything for you but I'm not without guilt." Bitsy felt something like conviction, a hard knot of insight and honesty, forming in her. "What I'm telling you now," she finished in a state close to intoxication, "is if you want me you will have to risk damnation."

Chuck shrugged, and though he didn't put it exactly this way, what he meant when he proposed was that there was risk to everything worthy of desire and that after nearly two decades on the wrong track, he'd grown tired enough of his public life to make the break he'd always dreamed of, roll his Levi's up another inch and begin, if Bitsy would with him, living a little more privately, guided by natural rhythms and empty of fear. After that it was only a matter of time, during which they made love at odd and exuberant angles, consulted maps and almanacs, and pooled their resources, before Chuck and Bitsy found themselves on a dusty plot of land they had purchased sight unseen and on the verge of arguing in front of a flowering century plant.

"You promised," Bitsy said, "I could have a garden. But that's a dry riverbed we just drove across."

"Today they're irrigating," Chuck explained. "There will be water tomorrow."

"So what about access? Don't we have access?"

"In a manner of speaking," Chuck said. "It's just that when the river's high we park and wade across it."

"And if it gets too high?"

"It won't. This is the desert. But look, in an emergency there is a bridge two miles down. You'd have to cut fences to get there, but I'm talking emergencies, Bitsy. We're not planning emergencies, are we?"

Bitsy squatted and thrust her hand into the sandy earth, which was hot and dry and pebbly for several inches beneath the surface. For her, the gamble was just to go far enough away. If she went far enough away, she believed, the necessity to balance what was noble and abstract against the hard requirements of daily life would be diminished and perhaps eliminated altogether. The back of her neck felt singed by the sun and as she reached to shield it she knew the clear choice was between either doubt or elation.

She said, "Where are the children going to play?"

Chuck said, "In the shade of the cottonwoods I'll plant by the river. Trust me."

Bitsy stayed her bet, and in the three years they lived there Chuck's cottonwoods grew to the height of her waist and she herself came to believe in a tall cool grove of them there someday. On the hottest days she would often imagine their refuge, children perhaps splashing in the water just beyond, a clay pitcher of lemonade beside her. And yes, she agreed with her husband that a treehouse was in order. These were little tricks of mind that afforded her, in their plain life, with great pleasure, but they were also acts of faith of the kind, and Bitsy knew this, that would never come easily to her mother.

4

♦ ♦ ♦

When the snow changed to rain, Bitsy slipped uneasily out of sleep and reached for Chuck at her side, but he was gone. It was a hard rain, noisy on the tile roof, just as the snow had been heavy. There was also, that late in the night, the slow grate of her mother's breathing and the soft, intermittent shifting of her daughter. From outside, too, there came an occasional plaintive bleating, like the honk of large, circling birds but low down to the ground and much sadder. After the silence of three days of snow, the night itself seemed noisy and full of prescience, if only Bitsy could penetrate it. As it was, she felt relieved the goats were safe and assumed, since Chuck had not returned, that he'd gone to help the neighbors: but who, she wondered, and on which side of the river?

Almost Bitsy envied him his urgent trek out into that dark night. She herself, listening to the rain, longed to thrust her arms into her cold, stiff parka, cinch her boots, and duck her head against the icy slash of rain, striding out through the knee-deep snow and taking action. On such a night, the space around her, wet and crackling softly where the elements converged, would feel almost alive and half dangerous. Before Clara, Bitsy would have gone with Chuck, and after the goats were safe, or the garden covered against frost, or the truck securely parked across the river, after they had made their cold way back and calmed themselves on whiskey warmed with lemon and a touch of honey, after they had washed the mud off and stoked the fire and made their way to bed, then they would find themselves charged by the physics of love, sometimes all the way until dawn. Before her mother, she would at least have got up anyway and lit the lamps and waited. But tonight, against all instinct, Bitsy forced herself to remain quiet and wait the night out tangled in her empty bed and wondering how, for all its recent activity, her life had worked itself around to this debilitating stasis.

In some ways it was so simple. From the time her father died to the time her aimlessness had sent her out to hear the poets talk against the war, Bitsy had balanced two lives against each other, keeping her mother fed, clothed, and bathed, while at the same time managing to stay in school, despair of the future, make love. It was never an easy balance and certainly there were trade-offs, but Bitsy, in perfecting the principle of separation, had preserved herself discrete from everything and thereby whole. With Chuck, she saw in retrospect, she lost her sense of boundaries, thus linking the first heady rise of desire in herself to the constant threat of dispersal.

Her mother seemed to relish it. "I'm warning you, Bitsy, he'll desert you when you need him. That's how men are. They're fickle; they die." Whereas Chuck seemed so healthy, so strong. Bitsy remembers him, that night he met her mother, worrying little pink packets of sugar in the cafe they went to later. His blunt-ended fingers toyed and toyed with the fragile paper. Her mother might as well have said: *Why are you taking my daughter from me? Why are you doing this to me?* And Chuck just sat there calmly, drinking his coffee, spilling sugar.

Thus, though when she went with him she hoped to make a decent claim on life, there was still a small matter of deception, of guilt, she had not yet resolved, not yet even faced. Bitsy knew this, just as she knew in her heart that the gamble was a bad one, that she could never go far enough away, that the time eventually would come when she would rise at dawn each day to tend to Clara first before her mother would need water, would need to be assisted from her cot, would need to be carried up hill to the privy. And Bitsy also knew that having come to this, eventually they would come as well to a night when snow would change to rain and Chuck, in the middle of the night, would leave her side, leaving her alone to make the morning coffee and try to explain to her mother in his absence the consequences of a rapid thaw.

"Where's Chuck?" she said when finally it was dawn. "I need the privy."

Bitsy folded the covers back and, lifting her mother's legs over the edge of the wood frame, helped her sit. Then Bitsy's mother grabbed hold of Bitsy's shoulders and the two of them hoisted her body to the nearby wheelchair. It was a routine they had perfected through years of repetition. Bitsy remembers half staggering under her mother's weight when she was small. She remembers, in adolescence, a feeling of repulsion at the uselessness of her mother's limbs. Later, in college, she lost patience.

"It's not even in style, Mother," she remembers saying once. "Get an eating disorder if you have to get something, but walk, for God's sake. Let my father rest in peace."

Now, as they faced each other once again inside the cold adobe, Bitsy saw it was herself who had craved peace, and looking about her, acknowledged for the first time the lengths she had gone to get it. What she had not anticipated was the lengths to which her mother, too, was willing to go to deny her.

"I asked you, where's Chuck?" her mother repeated. "I have my dignity, you know. Don't make me ask again."

Bitsy gestured a bit vaguely toward the windows, the gray, sopping day outside. It was worse than she had feared, with the surface of the snow giving way all over, leaving collections of water, some as large as small ponds, that continued to deepen and spread.

She said, "But Mother, it's raining."

"Snow, rain. What's next, young lady?"

"Don't, Mother," she said.

"A helluva place..."

"I'm warning you."

"...you brought me to, Bitsy."

There was a silence, during which Clara's cooing seemed loud. Bitsy drew a deep breath, then, inconsequentially, shrugged. "Nobody brought you, you came," she said. "As for your problem, use the chamber pot. We do."

Much later in the day, when the telephones were out and Chuck still had not returned and the river below had encroached into its flood plain and was still rising and Bitsy had gone out to feed the goats and come back soaked, her mother, as if she'd just begun to understand the situation, put down her book and laughed out loud, low and somewhat pleased in the corner, to herself. Bitsy took her wet clothes off and hung them by the stove. She put on dry jeans and one of Chuck's worn flannel shirts. Then she checked Clara and, finding her wet, changed her too. Each of her movements was deliberate, restrained. In each of them, she avoided even turning toward the south-facing wall, where the expanse of windows made an unstable boundary between that world outside and this one, Bitsy thought, inside.

Clara was restless, so Bitsy walked with her from one end of the house to the other, comforted by her daughter's warm and snug body against her chest. She avoided, too, turning toward her mother who, from time to time, still seemed to derive some special enjoyment from the weather and their predicament. Bitsy didn't think her mother fully grasped the extent of that predicament, but she wasn't saying anything either. From one end of the house to the other, she walked with her daughter. In the whole day, she wondered, how far could she walk? By counting steps, she might arrive at some approximate calculation. She was counting steps. By counting steps, she could keep herself from wondering where, in fact, Chuck had gone; she could shut out the thought of her mother; she could, with real effort, refrain from weighing the treachery of love against the treachery of nature. It was as if that other world were melting into this one. With Chuck gone—maybe to the neighbors, maybe, at last, into the hills—Bitsy half believed it was up to her to keep them both from melting down altogether.

In the end, not even Bitsy anticipated how quickly the river would rise, surging higher by several feet, it seemed, an hour and usurping the frail claims they and the others had made along it. At first the brown surge of water, its violent surface inscribed by huge, swirling whorls, carried only deadwood, an occasional tire, the usual debris of the river bank, but then a whole abandoned car washed by, and then a forest service sign and some cows. As Bitsy, compelled, now stood a kind of watch, she felt amazed by the ease with which the water swept its flotsam along like tiny pieces of foam. She began to recognize wreckage.

Still, the spectacle was entirely contained by the flood plain. If the flood plain could continue to contain it, Bitsy thought, they might wait out the storm unscathed. She thought about the turning tide, the languorous curl of receding waters. She thought how later she would tell it, how Chuck would knead her shoulders, sigh, kiss her neck, and tell her how much he had worried. She considered the benevolence of sunlight.

Between this way of thinking and the instant the water crested its bank, all the buttressing Bitsy had placed between herself and the necessity for action eroded. In that same instant, she turned away from the window. She felt stunned, but intent on convincing her mother exactly how things stood. If her mother could be convinced, Bitsy herself, she believed, would know what to do next.

But her mother, too, had been waiting, and before Bitsy could say *we're going to go now, Mother, we're going to drive cross-country to the bridge,* June unlocked her wheelchair and, working it toward Bitsy, said, "I told you he'd desert you. Now he's deserted you." She said it with some satisfaction and just the suspicion of a smile. And it was that smile, the half silly, half willful play of it at the corners of her mother's mouth, that unnerved Bitsy so completely that when she said what she had to say it was lamely and without conviction. Still smiling, her mother said, "But it's raining."

Bitsy looked helplessly at her mother and felt like crying. These were odds she hadn't counted on. Where was Chuck? How high could the river really go?

When she looked again, it was beginning to churn around the base of Chuck's cottonwoods. There was something calming in that. The little tree trunks seemed so sturdy. They would put a stand against it; they would stop it. But even as she thought it, it was as if all the water in the world were emptying into their inconstant river, and first the low boughs disappeared and then, as Bitsy watched, the very place where they had planned, someday, the treehouse, then one by one the trees gave way, ripped whole from the earth by the angry tide, then not Bitsy but Clara was crying, low and soft, crying and crying until, as the whole earth drained around them, Bitsy at last remembered she had a daughter now as well, no matter what, as a mother.

"Now, Mother," she heard herself saying. "I'm taking Clara to the truck and when I get back, I want you to be ready."

"Don't use that tone of voice with me," her mother said.

"I'll use whatever voice I want. We're out of vegetables. Chuck will want his whiskey. There's two miles of muck between us and that bridge, and if you're not coming now, you're staying here."

Even so, it wasn't easy getting the wailing Clara ready while June protested petulantly and outside the flood continued to worsen.

"I refuse," she said. "What's the point? Where's your husband when you need him? He's left you, like I said."

Bitsy worked her fingers up the tiny sleeve of Clara's jacket, groping for her hand which, clenched, had lodged itself somewhere near the middle. Clara screamed louder and kicked.

"You think it's easy staying here with you?" her mother said. "I'm doing it for you, you know. I never trusted him."

Bitsy crammed Clara's head into the hood and cinched the drawstring.

"But it's not my idea of a picnic, young lady."

Nor was it easy trudging with the baby through what was left of the snow—mostly mud now—up past the privy through the dripping orchard to the red Toyota truck which, four-wheel-drive or not, Bitsy was not all that certain would make it. By the time she returned to the house for her mother, she was completely splattered with mud, drenched, and not a little bit afraid.

"You never understood," her mother said. "You never even cared."

Bitsy closed the flue and glanced around the little house. Everywhere she was aware of Chuck, his earthy smell, the careful calculations of his mind, his hand. At least up in the hills it would be safe for him. But Bitsy didn't really think he'd gone into the hills.

"Don't come near me," her mother said. "I'm putting my foot down now."

"So put your foot down," Bitsy said. "Let me see you do it."

In the momentary silence that followed, neither woman was prepared for what Bitsy did next, slinging her mother over her shoulder and, though staggering a little at first as when she was small, plunging back out into the storm without even a shawl for her mother, no outer garments at all. At the first slash of rain, Bitsy felt her strength return, more than ever before, it seemed, and she worked with resolve, slipping only once in the ankle deep mud and anchoring her mother, who felt as light and inconsequential as someone else's recalcitrant child, firmly at her shoulder, both arms linked at the wrists. Still, it was hard work and she was breathing heavily when she thrust her mother unceremoniously as a sack of feed into the truck and hoisted herself in beside her.

"Hold the baby," she said. "There isn't time for the carseat."

"My wheelchair," her mother said.

"Good christ, Mother, we'll rent one in town."

But when Bitsy looked at her mother, she saw, for the first time in her life, what looked like tears. *If only she cried when my father died,* Bitsy thought. *She could have cried instead.* When she paused to think like that, the roar of the river was louder than anything she had ever heard. "Please," her mother said. Next to the sound of the river, the single word, uttered with such pathos, was the tiniest whisper, easy enough to slip through this world unheard, except—and Bitsy could not keep from looking—for those tears. *Shed a single tear,* she thought, *and I'll do anything for you.* It came as an almost brutal surprise, this love she felt for her mother, who, drenched and shivering, sat helplessly on the seat beside her, hugging Bitsy's now curious daughter tight to her chest and quietly crying.

Thus, Bitsy could have had no way of comprehending what happened as, charged with emotion and fatigue, she rushed back from the house with the wheelchair, nor even, I would imagine, of registering what she must have seen when the red Toyota truck, as if imbued with a will of its own, revved high, ground gears, and, jolting into motion, came at her through the trees, skidding in the mud, but unavoidable.

5

♦ ♦ ♦

The elements, I warned you when we started, are, and will remain, in disjunction. This is the way of things, and though you would perhaps have preferred that I had arranged them in some kind of harmony—put a bathroom in, at least, or made the flood plain wider—we would then have been working with lies, and though this is fiction, there's no room for lies. If it had been up to me, I swear it, I'd have been happy enough to leave the little valley to itself, but Chuck had other ideas, and Bitsy had her past, she had her inconsolable future. Should we then hold it against her that she desired, like the rest of us, to be consoled and the hell with it? Clara never was an afterthought. She was born to a promise of life and deserves it. But even that is complicated. Probably, it is more complicated than everything else.

You will wonder, too, how it all turned out, the skid of that truck, Bitsy shielding herself with a collapsed wheelchair and a look of expectation so keen it almost seems like hope. There is so much mud it is hard to see, and the baby, Clara, is strangely silent. You can't help but wonder what she'd tell if she could speak. You can't help but wish someone would tell. But June isn't talking either, and if I were to tell you how she watched her daughter the way she might have watched a stranger who was somehow responsible for all the grief in her life, you would have no cause to trust me. June is an enigma to me. Like the baby Clara's, I can visualize her face but am unable to penetrate it. All I can tell you for certain is it was never by choice that she withdrew from the world. She had been, until her husband's death, a happy woman, vibrant and connected and with so much pride and joy in her daughter. Then, just like that, just like Bitsy in the storm, she was cut off from everything she loved or understood. If it took her thirty years to find a way back, when she found it, she found it with a vengeance. And maybe vengeance, finally, was the right response; or maybe that wasn't it at all. Whatever it was, it was something June herself could never articulate in words but which her body, as if in a dream, remembered with a precise, uncanny compulsion. This was not something she willed, it just happened: the way, after all those years, power returned like an instinct to her legs; the way her feet sought and found and worked the pedals of an unfamiliar truck as skillfully as if she had been driving all her life; the way, after that surge of omnipotence and fury, the legs resumed their lameness, and the baby, beside her, started screaming.

It is this exact instant, pierced by the infant's frantic wail, that has, I must confess, intrigued me all along; and yet, having arrived here at last, I find I am unable to bring it into focus for you. I know it is a matter of perspective, but if we draw back some to get a little distance, you will naturally wonder about that man signaling toward Bitsy's house from the other side of the river. Is it Chuck? He is wearing rolled Levi's and an old canvas parka, but they all, in this part of the country, wear their Levi's rolled and old parkas. Still, the man seems intent, wild, almost. And yes, he does seem to be trying to gesture that—what, the bridge is down? Well I know for a fact that the bridge is down, but from that far away the man himself is just a tiny speck and the red Toyota truck barely big enough to see through the trees, when what you really want is to draw closer, closer even than before, close enough to see in and to hear what Bitsy's lame mother is saying to the shrieking baby beside her, for in her pitiful efforts to comfort the child, she keeps patting at the clenched and flailing fist and over and over repeating, "Don't worry, your mother's not hurt. Your mother doesn't know the first thing about pain. She's fine, don't worry. She's just making a fuss, a fuss about nothing. Nothing, my child. Nothing at all."

Carla Tomaso

♦

Tattoo

"HURRY UP," Eleanor shouts at my bedroom window. She is outside loading the car and I am taking my time fixing my hair which is thin and needs a lot of work. Ten minutes before this the zipper on my pants broke so I had to start all over again getting dressed, which meant I had to repack my suitcase as well. Not a good omen, any of this, for beginning a two-week vacation with someone you've never traveled with before. I glance once around my bedroom with exaggerated nostalgia as if this is the last time I'll ever see it. Then I begin to wonder why I go anywhere. I'm anxious for a week before the departure date; it takes me four days to adjust to the new place and, when I get home, I invariably get sick.

But Eleanor is standing in my doorway now, smoking a cigarette. She is short with a round freckled face and lavishly curly gray hair. She is not afraid of anything. She has been married three times and has a tattoo on her wrist that she got on her last vacation. Supposedly it didn't hurt. It's of a butterfly because she's a Gemini, Eleanor has explained, and Geminis ride the breeze. I take that to mean that she doesn't stay with any one thing too long. She had it put on her wrist so she can cover it with the face of her watch when she's at work (she's an ophthalmologist not far from the university where I'm in administration). We met at a meeting of Adventuring Women, a group that organizes outdoor vacations for women who, for whatever reason, don't want to be with men. Eleanor's reason is that she is sick of them.

"Now hurry up, Nikki, or we'll hit the commuter traffic," she says. I'm moving slower than usual because it's so early in the morning and Eleanor is making me nervous.

"The zipper on my pants broke," I say. "Maybe we shouldn't go." As soon as I say it, I want to take it back. Eleanor's mouth twitches, just slightly, but enough to let me see I've hurt her feelings. "Oh, you know how neurotic I am," I tell her. "Don't pay attention to anything I say." I hate to belittle myself just to make Eleanor feel better, but it seems easier than telling her the truth, which is that I'm scared to spend a whole two weeks alone with her. We have a pretty nice friendship as it is; we talk on the phone once a week and take long walks in the mountains on weekends when it isn't rainy. Why push it? Spending a lot of time together is only asking for trouble. I'm a lesbian and she's not so there's no romance, thank God. And no judgments either. She once said to me, "I envy you. Going to bed with a man is just plain stupid."

"Carry this, would you?" I say and hand Eleanor the Sportsac garment bag I bought for the trip. We're taking her car, a comfortable but small gray Toyota, so I've had to decide carefully what I'll need. I hand her the bag but I don't let go when she tries to take it. I stare into her green eyes for a couple of seconds. I notice for the first time that her left eye seems to be more brown than green and I wonder crazily if this dysymmetry is what caused her to go into ophthalmology. She returns the look but then realizes her cigarette is burning her fingers and turns to find an ashtray.

"What the hell is wrong with you today?" she says, finally just grabbing the bag from me. "You having your period? I hope not. It's a mess bleeding on a vacation with hotel sheets and gas stations. I'm glad I'm through with all that shit." She walks downstairs to her car with my bag over her shoulder. The bottom hangs practically to the ground.

Everything in my bedroom, except for a pair of sheepskin slippers, is put away. I decide to leave them out so I can think of them, while we're hundreds of miles up the coast, waiting for me to come home. I walk downstairs and check all the doors and then go outside where Eleanor has just finished packing the trunk.

"You want me to drive?" I say to Eleanor who puts my suitcase in the backseat. "Wait. You like to drive, don't you?"

"Yeah," Eleanor says, getting into the driver's seat. I climb into the other side and put my seat belt on.

"Should I run back in the house and get some apples or water?" I ask her. "I didn't even think of it."

She starts the motor. "Don't worry about it," she says. I can see the butterfly on her wrist because she's not wearing her watch today.

"It hasn't faded at all," I say. The wings are bluish green and the body is red, outlined in black. It really looks like it belongs there, like it's a miraculous freak of pigmentation, not something put on with a needle.

"You ought to get one," she says. "A crescent moon, maybe, or a scorpion. That's what you are, right?"

"What?" I say.

"Sign of the zodiac," she says. She speeds up to get through the yellow light and I push down on the floorboard with both feet.

"Yeah, November," I say. "I'm supposed to be sexy and vindictive. Fiercely demanding of loyalty."

"Where'd you find all that out?" she asks, like it's funny I should know that stuff.

"Somebody gave me a birthday card with it written on the inside." Actually I'm pretty interested in astrology and I like being a Scorpio, even though I think I act more like a Libra.

"We couldn't be worse for each other," Eleanor says, laughing. "This vacation we're going to get you tattooed." The way she says it makes me feel like a head of range cattle. "You're going to come back from this vacation with a beautiful work of art on your butt," she says.

"Why my butt?" I say. All I can think of is the time my mother got me vaccinated and it hurt so much I didn't speak to her for three days afterwards.

"Why not?" Eleanor says, merging neatly into the slow lane of traffic. "It's as good a place as any and it doesn't show, unless..." she looks at me and winks. I think it's kind of mean to bring that up when she knows for a fact that it's been two full years since I've been to bed with anybody.

"But it's so permanent," I say. I'd heard they could take off tattoos but I knew the outline would still be there no matter what they did. "What if I change my mind later?" I can't imagine anyone wanting to tamper with their body. It's like saying you're God.

Eleanor runs her butterfly hand through her curly hair. "I think you should get a crescent moon with a little star in the concave part," she says, finally. "That fits you just right."

Eleanor drives as if we are in a tremendous hurry and after a couple of hours of strained reminiscences about terrible family vacations we stop at an ARCO for a fill-up and the bathroom Eleanor buys a Mounds bar and I get a soft ice cream cone even though it's only 10:00 in the morning. Then we get back in the car and start driving again. I begin to feel better about going on vacation. I pretend we're on our way to take a spring hike.

We talk about this woman, Roberta, whom we know from our first Adventuring Women canoe trip. The thing about her is that she just married a man, and on the canoe trip she was so homesick for a woman that the leader had to canoe her seven hours back to the parking lot where we had left our cars. Eleanor thinks it's a lot weirder than I do but that's probably because she's so off men at the moment. I almost ask Eleanor if she's ever had any homosexual inclinations but I decide we're on a vacation together for two weeks and why get into that?

At about noon we pass an old tourist attraction I remember driving by when I was a kid and we were going on vacation. It was a family-type restaurant, as I recall, and in front there was a recreation area for kids with slides that ran through the bodies of giant fiberglass animals. Sort of like a McDonalds but bigger. For example, if you climbed up the elephant's back, you entered the slide at its head and shot out through the trunk. All that's left is an empty lot with a two-story gray-green dinosaur standing in the middle. Part of the dinosaur's skin has fallen off and I can see the wooden framing inside. Before I think to tell Eleanor we've sped past it. She's going seventy-five.

Finally Eleanor takes us to a truck stop restaurant. Without warning, she just pulls off the highway and into the parking lot like that was our exact destination all along. It is 4:30 in the afternoon and we're only an hour or so from the cabin we've rented on the edge of the Pacific Ocean. "I'm sick of driving," she says, "and I want some onion rings." We climb out of the car and stretch our backs. Eleanor lights her second cigarette of the day. She always seems to know what she wants, which probably made it both easy and hard on all her husbands. I admire her for it. I hardly ever know what I want; all the possibilities have so many sides.

"You've been very nice about not smoking," I say. I put my arm around her and we walk into the restaurant. There's a good solid feel to her, and because she's about three inches shorter than I am, it's a little like she's holding me up.

"I don't notice so much when I'm driving," she says, dragging deeply.

We sit down at a booth next to the window and order cokes and onion rings and just as the waitress is walking away, repeating our order to herself as she finishes jotting it down, Eleanor calls to her, "Make that to go, would you?" The waitress, a large woman with jet-black hair the color of a piano stool, turns around and glares at us. The management has dressed her in a pink fifties waitress uniform that hits above her dimpled knees and makes her look like a joke. I think she is worried about her tip but when Eleanor smacks down two dollars she seems satisfied and takes our order to the kitchen.

"I don't like this place," Eleanor says. "Too many men." I look around for the first time and notice about a dozen men, a couple at tables talking, but most of them solemnly smoking and drinking coffee at the counter, not even looking our way.

"Oh, come on," I say to her. "Nobody gives a shit. Please let's stay in here. I'm just beginning to get over the sensation that we're still moving."

"I suppose you like the artwork," Eleanor says, lighting another cigarette. She points at the wall where a blonde dressed in a black bikini two sizes too small for her is drinking water from a garden hose. The cashier, a small, dark-haired woman, is ringing up a paunchy truck driver directly beneath the woman's rear end. "How would you like to be strung up like that, like so much meat?" she says.

"Of course I don't like it," I say, "but I'm on vacation and I don't want to get all worked up about every little sexist thing we run into." I lean back on the bench and feel proud of myself for saying exactly what I want to. I'd gone through a period of feminist rage a couple of years before and now, probably because of exhaustion, I've trained myself to look straight through the billboards and magazine ads and everything else, like they're all just so much stale air.

"Little sexist thing!" Eleanor shouts. "Let's leave," she says and begins to stand up.

"No," I say, "please." I must be giving her just the right look because she stamps out her cigarette and then walks over and says something to the waitress. "Thanks," I say when she sits back down.

"Want to play a game?" she says. "Want to see how long it takes one of these assholes to get up and come over here and try to join us?"

"That won't happen, Eleanor," I say. "Everybody's tired. It's 5:00 on a Monday afternoon and all anybody can think about is getting home."

"They're thinking about sex and trashing women, take my word for it." She taps the table a few times with her index finger for emphasis.

"I hate the way you do that," I say.

"I've been around a lot longer than you and I've known a lot more men." She pauses. "And they're all the same."

"So what's it matter how many I've known if they're all the same?" I say. At this moment, the waitress returns with our onion rings and two glasses of water.

"You decided to stay," she says. "Good idea. The Interstate gets real bad at this hour. Last night on top of everything else somebody's car flipped over and burned up. We were stuck for ninety minutes without moving and I'm claustrophobic." She takes a bottle of ketchup out of her apron pocket and puts it next to the onion rings.

Eleanor bites into an onion ring and I begin to think about how you never know what people are going to come up with to be crazy about. Here is this perfectly normal looking waitress who hates closed-in spaces. "So what did you do," I ask her, "about the traffic jam?"

"Oh, I just got out of the car and walked around it a few times," she says. "It helped that I knew I wasn't really trapped. I mean I could've just left the car there and run down the off ramp any time I felt like it."

And Eleanor with her thing about men. And me with my...what? My phobia about being with anybody for more than a few hours at a time?

The waitress leaves and Eleanor pushes the plate of onion rings at me. She has already made quite a dent. "What are you thinking about?" she asks me.

"My parents," I say.

"Oh," she says. "Forget it." I take an onion ring from the plate and curve it through the little mound of ketchup Eleanor's put on the side. "I thought you might be homesick," she says, real seriously. I can't tell if she's making fun of me or not so I let it go. The truth is just at this moment I am missing my two cats who are probably staring squinty-eyed out of their cages at the cat hotel where I took them last night. I'd tried to tell the night manager their personalities but she looked so bored I just sort of trailed off and left the phone number of our cabin.

"She didn't bring our cokes," Eleanor says.

"I'll catch her eye," I say, for some reason feeling responsible. I turn around to see where the waitress is and I notice that the man three booths behind us is staring in our direction. Because there's nobody in the booths between us, he sees me looking and glances down at his plate. The top of his head is bald in a perfect circle about the circumference of an English muffin. I think of a target. "I don't see her anywhere," I say. "Just drink the water for now. She's bound to come over this way soon."

Eleanor is nervous about getting the cokes, as if she's worried about losing money on them or something. She smokes a cigarette with one hand and eats an onion ring with the other. I can tell she's not thinking about anything except where are those cokes.

"These are good," I say, biting into another onion ring. The batter is light and crispy and the onion tastes sweet.

"People write guidebooks about the best diner food to buy on vacation," Eleanor says, looking over to the cash register to see if the waitress is there. Then she puts her cigarette out.

"You on vacation?" a voice says. The balding man has suddenly appeared at the end of our table.

"No," Eleanor says, not even looking up. It's as if she sensed that he was on his way over. There is a silence. The man is trying to size us up. Not in a mean or sly way, but just if he should ask something else or go. Finally he smiles at Eleanor.

"Yes, you are," he says. "I heard you talking about vacations as I was passing by. I'm on vacation, too."

"She lives a couple of miles south of here and I live a couple of miles north. We meet once a week for onion rings halfway in between," Eleanor says. Now she's looking at him with her jaws clamped together tight.

The man continues smiling at both of us. He has lovely large white teeth. He's wearing a light blue cashmere pullover and gray corduroy slacks and he reminds me of a guest conductor or a psychiatrist, definitely not a masher. I can't understand why Eleanor's putting us all through this.

"That was really an untruth," she says, straight at his white teeth, "intended to blow you away. We have all the company we need."

"I'm sorry," the man says. "I was just on my way to pay the bill and I heard 'vacation' so I thought we might exchange notes. I'm heading north to escape the smog for a month."

Suddenly the waitress comes up behind him, smiling, as if she's terrifically pleased to find him there. She has the cokes. "I forgot your cokes," she says, moving around him so she can put them on the table in front of us. "Am I too late?" she says.

"Yes," Eleanor says and nods at the plate of onion rings, which is empty.

"Are you joining them?" the waitress says to the man. "You want her coke?" and she puts one coke in front of my place and one to my right where he would be sitting. Then she puts the bill on the table. "Tell the cashier to take the cokes off the bill if you don't want them," she says and goes to check on another table.

"We're leaving now," Eleanor says, standing up.

"Of course," the man says. "I'm Don Peterson." He walks with us to the cash register. I stand to the side while Eleanor pays. I notice that she doesn't tell the cashier to take the cokes off the bill. "People always say that diners have the best food," Don says, waiting to pay behind Eleanor. "Somebody even wrote a guidebook about it."

I begin to feel sorry for Don Peterson and ashamed of Eleanor for treating him so badly. I begin to think that there's something wrong with me for being her friend. "Sounds lonely," I say to him, out of the blue, and he looks at me as if he doesn't remember who I am.

"What?" he says. Eleanor glares at me fiercely but I can't stop now.

"Going up north by yourself, to get out of the smog."

"It's what I want to do," he says, and leaves it at that.

Don Peterson has a convertible Mercedes and it is parked next to Eleanor's Toyota. "My one extravagance," he says, patting the door. "I've always hated the heavy libidinal thing Americans have for their cars but it's heaven to drive." Then he gets in, backs it out and waves at us. "Have a nice vacation," he shouts out the window as if nothing has happened, as if he just had a delightful talk with two women he'd never met before. We get in Eleanor's car and follow him out onto the surface road.

Eleanor is driving much slower than she was before we stopped. She merges into the middle lane of the freeway and stays there. Don Peterson's Mercedes is about five cars in front of us. "Men think we should be grateful for the interruption," she says. I look straight ahead. A huge bug splatters its guts on the windshield just my side of center. I stare at the yellow and red goo. Eleanor doesn't talk for a while, which is just as well because I can't seem to decide how I feel about anything.

Finally I look over toward Eleanor and it's like she's punched me in the throat because she's crying. Not hard, but just enough that the tears are falling down her cheek and landing on her blue cotton shirt. I look away and stare at the squashed bug on the windshield, wondering what the hell I should say. I've never seen her cry before.

From the right, a four-wheel drive jeep, license plate TOUGH, cuts in front of us. I shout "Watch out!" just in time and Eleanor slams on the brakes.

"Jesus," she says. "The waitress was sure right about the traffic."

"Eleanor," I say.

"What?" she says. She's stopped crying but there are still little puddles of tears caught under her eyes. "You want to change your tampax? I did sort of rush us out of the restaurant fast."

"No," I say. "Actually I don't even have my period."

"I thought you said you did." she says. "I've been under that impression all day."

"I've decided to get the tattoo," I say.

"Hot damn," she says. "If we go down to the boardwalk right when we get into town, it'll have time to heal while we're still up here. We'll buy some Vaseline at the drugstore."

"But you got yours someplace else," I say, trying to remember where she went for vacation last year.

"That's okay. These places have to be licensed. Besides, I'll check out the equipment, to see that it's sterile and all that. I won't let anything bad happen to you."

She turns toward me for a moment and one of the old tears slips down her cheek. She wipes it off with the back of her hand and smiles.

Suddenly I feel dangerously euphoric. The sensation sweeps over me that from now on all the messes in my life are going to be as just as easy to fix as this one. I say, "Well, get going," and without any hesitation she merges into the fast lane and all of a sudden, at seventy-five miles an hour, we're flying past everybody on the road.

Gita B. Carlstrom

◆

Hit the Beat

I WATCH ANNA doing her act on stage, and wonder if she's laying it on especially for my benefit. I just met her; we smoked a joint in her car before we came in.

"So what do you think?" she asked, holding her breath.

I let mine out, explosively, and took another hit. "Tastes nice." Nod in appreciation, and pass it back. "Thanks."

"Not the weed, dummy." She blew smoke in my face. "The job."

"It's okay, pretty nine to five. And I think I'm improving."

"Improving?" She held out the doob.

"No more for me, thanks. Yeah, I notice some of the girls can really dance, it's nice. I feel so clumsy, I'd like to be more like them."

"You would?"

"Yeah. I mean, it's all very well to just get up there and be gross, but I'd rather be more professional about it, if possible."

"Mmmmm," she said. "I see." Then she put the joint out and just got out of the car.

So now I feel like a damn idiot. I sit at the bar with a Coke, and watch Anna peel out of her kimono. She spreads it out on the stage, reclines, and languidly fans herself for five full minutes. Twisting slightly back and forth, she displays her long fine limbs and porcelain, hairless skin. Pulling the chopstick from her topknot, she shakes out her curtain of hair; black, straight and falling to her ass.

"Viva!" she calls, "a shot glass!"

I blush fiercely, but here in the dark nobody sees.

A man in a hunting jacket plucks the glass from my fingers. Handing it to her he sinks into his seat, transfixed.

Anna has punched up five top forty songs—the kind that all run into one another. This song is about love, or betrayal. Slowly, she licks the entire inside of the glass. It is like watching a kiss, from the inside.

More men are moving to the front, and I'm alone at the bar with Chuck, the owner. I worked for him once as a waitress. He is not surprised to see me.

"So you're back," he says. "How long?"

"Couple of weeks." I smile. "How's it going?"

He reaches over the bar for a beer. "Same old. You know how it is." He drinks, smacks his lips, snorts. "Dancers."

Anna inclines her head, and with her left hand pushes her right breast to her lips. Her pointed tongue darts out and circles and stabs at the nipple. Raising her gaze, she slides the shot glass down. In the glass, the great brown eye of her breast is rimmed with tears.

This song is about a little bit of heart and soul.

Her long red fingernails scratch and flick the supine length of her body. Her pelvis twists. The stage is at eye level. A man with bristly hair fingers currency; his hands, mechanically rubbing the paper, come away dirty. Another, in a John Deere cap, grips his drink for strength. Even the ones that come together avoid each other's eyes.

Anna's hand closes around the glass. Norah, behind the bar, sighs heavily. "Not again," she breathes, and goes into the walk-in for another case of beer.

Chuck turns abruptly, knocking over my soda. "No flashing!" he barks.

Too late. Anna has already swallowed the glass, and is re-tying her G string. She smiles like a cat and, dressing, moves gracefully around the stage. When Chuck bends to mop up the soda, she opens the kimono and expels the glass into Bristly Hair's waiting hand. He slips his nervous money into the pocket of her robe.

On her way to the dressing room she gives me that feline smile—all wide red mouth, no eyes at all.

"Good luck," she says.

Everybody drives around to the bar to re-up; there hasn't been a waitress since I quit. There weren't any tips anyway. John Deere offers me a drink, but it'll have to wait.

Chuck grabs my arm on my way up the steps. "You know the rules," he says. "I'll thank you to watch your ass in my club."

I laugh. After that performance, I'll probably be the only one who does.

My routine is a little more standard. Lip-sync, strip, dance, dress. Maybe a little floor work in the fifth song, if the cash looks forthcoming. Actually, I do have one trick up my sleeve.

Split the bottom of a cardboard match with your fingernail, about halfway up. Moisten the resulting little crotch with your tongue. Grasp a nipple between two fingers; roll until firm, and perch the whole arrangement thereon. When both are set up, take a casual drag of a patron's cigarette, and touch the business end to the sulfur heads. Happy Birthday!

You won't get burned, remember—the matches are wet. If the customer blows them out, it's good for twenty bucks, at least.

I lie on the stage with my feet on the rail and toss my body around. The faces framed in the vee of my legs are slack with waiting. I slide my finger cautiously under my waistband.

"I said no flashing, damn it!"

Flipping over, I raise my rear in the air and flatten my chest to the stage. I get the sawbuck, anyway.

When I come down John Deere is waiting for me. I accept his offer of a drink. Anna approaches the stage with a box of Fig Newtons. It's going to get crazy in here tonight.

This song is about going home.

Between sets I drink golden tequila with salt and lemon, and play pool. Some bikers come in with a Doberman and lay out lines on the bar. I'd like to join them, but Norah stops me.

"Don't do that. How do you know what you're putting into your body?"

Anna is doing her stuff with the Fig Newtons, auctioning them off. I put my tips in my G string, or in the ankle strap of my spike heeled shoes. Anna's lie crumpled on the stage. It's all a matter of style.

Between the joint and the shots, I'm feeling pretty mellow. I pop my contact lenses for the next set. Surrounded by the red bordello haze of lights, I practice my belly rolls. I can't see anything too clearly and I'm afraid of falling off the stage.

The bikers open a space for me between them at the bar. There are more lines there. Norah glares at us. One of them, the one with the dog, shakes some more coke out on the bar. "Don't worry," he leers, "I'll be your taster."

John Deere asks me to play some pool. The curve of my body fits into his as he leans over my stance. They all want to teach you the game.

The break goes wild. "Stripes or solids?"

His arms reach around mine and our hands enfold the cue. I slide the stick back and forth and take aim. His mustache grazes my neck, then ear.

"I like the way you look up there," he whispers. "Can you come outside with me?" His breath is hot against my shoulder. "Just for a minute?"

I shoot; nine ball in the side. He's ridiculous and I am drunk. "I have to work, but thanks anyway."

He presses his length into me. He is strong, maybe works in construction. "After?"

"Fifteen off the twelve, to the corner." Crack—the fifteen hovers near the pocket, stops. I relinquish the cue. "Your shot."

He knocks off the rest of his colors, then blows it with the eight ball. "I'll pay you."

I hit five fast songs on the juke, and shake and shimmy my way through. Stay on my feet this time.

"Give 'em something, for Christ's sake," Chuck hisses at me, "what'm I paying you for?"

This round, Anna has a hand puppet.

He's waiting for me by the dressing room. His Deere hat is in his hand and his forehead is red and sweaty where the brim used to be

"So how about it?"

God, he's working it. I need to put some drops in my eyes, the smoke in here is killing me. I try to get past him, but he blocks the door.

"I'm serious, baby, I have three big ones here to prove it." He holds them up; six fifties, fresh from the bank, crackle in his palm. I don't know what to say. You can sit on that stage and do nothing, and there's those that'll hand you their entire paycheck, five dollars at a time. Sometimes you show them something, or let them graze you with their fingertips. Sometimes all you have to do is look them in the eye.

"Excuse me," I say, "there's something in my eye."

This song is about Funkytown.

"Look," he says, opening the door, "I'll leave the money here. Without entering, he reaches in and drops the money on the make-up table, then pulls the door shut behind him. "You think about it, right?" And goes back to the bar.

There are twenty minutes left of break. I fix my lenses, and step outside for some air. Looking up at the stars, I wonder what's going to happen.

Two more sets. It's late. I'm tired. John Deere is talking to Anna at the bar, but when I go to change my costume, the money is still on the table. It's a lot of money. I ask Norah what to do.

"I used to dance myself, you know." She wipes out some barware. "Think about what you're doing," she says, "really, think about it. Do what you can live with."

Anna asks me if I want to do the last set together. She's cleared it with Chuck; it'll be a nice piece of business, he says. Deere takes the front table as we approach the stage.

Anna breathes instructions to me while I wing it. Kneeling, I pull her stocking taut and hook it to her garter. We move past one another and each place a foot on the rail, crossing legs. The bachelor party sitting in the corner goes wild. She holds a shot glass to my breast; I hold a hand to hers. Stroking my waist, she gives a little push. Our hips roll together.

"I thought you didn't like me," I whisper.

"I thought you didn't like yourself." She bends me way back. Behind her long fall of hair, it will look like we're kissing. "You'll do fine," she says.

When we're done, the money will be gone from the dressing room. We'll smoke another joint, maybe, and count up our tips. We'll make enough, plenty, more than we ever could otherwise.

Bárbara Selfridge

◆

On Foot

W HO LOVES THE WORLD? You do. And does the world
love you? I don't know. It's hard, sometimes, to say yes.
Just like sometimes office temps can't afford their lunch hours,
and sometimes, after a day of file-clerking among well-dressed
strangers, they can't stand to go home. Better to lurk a while instead
in the silent, hidden rooms of the New York Public Library.

Even that luxury, though, turns too risky after dark, and this
particular file clerk—me—leaves the library quickly, hurrying to
the subway through the light drizzle of this particular nightfall.
New York is a city on foot, pedestrians more impervious to contact
than their car-enclosed counterparts. Walking, we enclose
ourselves by looking wholly disinterested in change.

Disinterest, however, is a look that children can't assume, and as
I walk past, I watch three of them play in front of the mica-flecked
lions. Three kids in hooded parkas, arms outstretched as they teach
themselves tight-rope walking and other important aspects of
five-year-old life.

I'm walking past, foot following foot across the flat gray slate of that city sidewalk, when suddenly I trip. All of me falls forward, all five-feet-four-inches, and only the heels of my palms stop my face from striking wet slate.

"Are you all right?"

A stranger comes from behind me, a man in a suit who reaches down to take my arm and help me up.

"I fell," I tell him.

Another man, one in a birghtly embroidered fez, rushes up. "Are you all right?"

I don't answer because I can't tell yet. My palms sting and a dark gray wetness drips off them like blood. "I fell down," I say.

"You tripped," says the man who helped me up.

"The rain makes everything slippery," says the other.

I look up and smile, they smile, and for a moment both men wait for me to say I'm all right.

But I swear they'd rather I wouldn't. They'd rather go on as they are: two openhearted men reaching out strong, capable hands to a fixable distress. Because this is the truth. Because quick before it disappears, this is the real truth: that office temp loves the world with all her heart and those two men, those two former children, would be so happy to help her right it.

Contributors' Notes

JULIA ALVAREZ was born in New York City and spent her early childhood in the Dominican Republic. She has been a scholar at the Bread Loaf Writers' Conference and has won an Academy of Poetry Prize, the Jenny McKean Moore Visiting Lectureship in Creative Writing from George Washington University for 1984-85 She is recipient of a General Electric Foundation Award, a PEN Syndicated Fiction Award, a Third Woman Press Award. She has been an assistant professor of English and Creative Writing at the University of Illinois. She is the author of *Homecoming* (Grove Press, 1984) and *The Housekeeping Book* and editor of *Old Age Ain't For Sissies*

DOROTHY BRYANT was born in San Francisco in 1930, the second daughter of immigrants from northern Italy. She has published eight novels with Northern California settings: *Ella Price's Journal, The Kin of Ata Are Waiting For You, Miss Giardino, The Garden of Eros, Prisoners, Killing Wonder, A Day in San Francicso,* and most recently, *Confessions of Madame Psyche.* Her short stories and essays are collected in *Myths to Lie By* and her one non-fiction book, *Writing a Novel,* is widely used in creative writing classes.

GITA CARLSTROM lives and works in lower Manhattan.

WINN GILMORE is, at the time of this publication, in Brazil, completing a collection of short stories she hopes to have published in 1988. She grew up in the 1960s and 70s in Birmingham, Alabama, in an extended family. After graduating from Smith College in 1984, she moved to California, where she still resides. She dedicates "Rev'ren Peach" to Juana Maria Rodriguez "in love and the awareness that words and knowledge are empowering. . . to those who dare to recognize it."

KATHARINE HAAKE'S first collection of stories, *No Reason on Earth*, was recently published by Dragon Gate Press (Port Townsend, WA). Her stories have appeared in *The Minnesota Review, Carolina Quarterly, New England Review* and *Bread Loaf Quarterly*. She teaches fiction at California State University, Northridge.

JENNIFER KREBS travels across the San Francisco Bay Bridge every day. While en route, she ponders the distance from her father's Holsteins in Spencerport, New York, to the Old Wives Tales Bookstore collective meeting, to the seminar in Urban Geography at San Francisco State University, to her lover's arms and cat's meows in Berkeley. It's a long way and she wishes she could drive like Shirley Muldowney.

MARNIE MUELLER'S short stories and poems have appeared in the *Croton Review, Xanadu, IKON, The Minnesota Review, Five Fingers Review, Painted Bride Quarterly, Real Fiction,* and *Between C & D.*

DEBORAH ROSE O'NEAL is a 1987 recipient of the PEN Syndicted Fiction Project award. Her stories have appeared and are scheduled for future publication in two anthologies as well as in *Northeast Magazine, New England Sampler, Pacific Review, Kansas Quarterly,* and *The Southern Review*. She lives in Connecticut with her husband, John, who is an elementary school teacher. She has two stepdaughters, Jennifer and Amy, and three sons, Seth, Aaron and Gabriel.

CANYON SAM lives in her hometown San Francisco. Her poetry, fiction, essays, and satire have appeared in numerous journals and periodicals including *Common Lives/Lesbian Lives, Feminary, Coming Up!,* and the award-winning anthology *New Lesbian Writing*. She is an activist for the Tibetan Nuns Project and the cause of Tibetan independence.

PATRICIA ROTH SCHWARTZ is a psychotherapist in private practice in the Boston area. She is also a writer, publishing fiction, poetry, non-fiction and reviews in women's and small press journals. Her volume of short fiction is forthcoming from New Victoria Publishers in Norwich, VT.

BÁRBARA SELFRIDGE has studied and been arrested with Grace Paley, also waitressed, pasted-up newspapers, and taught school. Her story, "The Divorce of Nydia Nevarez," appeared in the first issue of *The Caribbean Writer*, and won a Judith Siegel Pearson Award.

JOAN TOLLIFSON is in the master's program in Creative Writing at San Francisco State University and is currently at work on a novel. "Watering the Plants" is her first published fiction.

CARLA TOMASO lives in Southern California where she writes plays and stories when she is not teaching English. She graduated from Mount Holyoke College and went on to receive a master's in Creative Writing from Boston University. While at BU, she won the Gerald Warner Brace Award for the year's best short story. Her plays have been produced in the Los Angeles area and her stories have been published in *BACHY, Ploughshares* and *Common Lives/ Lesbian Lives*.

About the Editor:

LOUISE RAFKIN lives in Oakland, California, works evenings at a newspaper and is a student of Kajukenbo Kung Fu. Her articles and reviews have been widely published in magazines and newspapers, and her stories have appeared in literary journals. She has been honored by The National Gay and Lesbian Press Association for her Opinion and Commentary Writing, and "Blueprints for Modern Living" was a winner in *A Critique of America's* nationwide fiction contest. In 1987 she toured the country with her first book, *Different Daughters: A Book by Mothers of Lesbians* (Cleis Press), currently in its third printing.

♦ ♦ ♦

Books from Cleis Press

You Can't Drown the Fire: Latin American Women Writing in Exile edited by Alicia Partnoy. ISBN: 0-939416-16-6 24.95 cloth; ISBN: 0-939416-17-4 9.95 paper.

Unholy Alliances: New Fiction by Women edited by Louise Rafkin. ISBN: 0-939416-14-x 21.95 cloth; ISBN: 0-939416-15-8 9.95 paper.

Sex Work: Writings by Women in the Sex Industry edited by Frédérique Delacoste and Priscilla Alexander. ISBN: 0-939416-10-7 24.95 cloth; ISBN: 0-939416-11-5 10.95 paper.

Different Daughters: A Book by Mothers of Lesbians edited by Louise Rafkin. ISBN: 0-939416-12-3 21.95 cloth; ISBN: 0-939416-13-1 8.95 paper.

The Little School: Tales of Disappearance & Survival in Argentina by Alicia Partnoy. ISBN: 0-939416-08-5 21.95 cloth; ISBN: 0-939416-07-7 8.95 paper.

With the Power of Each Breath: A Disabled Women's Anthology edited by Susan Browne, Debra Connors & Nanci Stern. ISBN: 0-939416-09-3 24.95 cloth; ISBN: 0-939416-06-9 9.95 paper.

Voices in the Night: Women Speaking About Incest edited by Toni A.H. McNaron & Yarrow Morgan. ISBN: 0-939416-02-6 9.95 paper.

Long Way Home: The Odyssey of a Lesbian Mother & Her Children by Jeanne Jullion. ISBN: 0-939416-05-0 8.95 paper.

The Absence of the Dead Is Their Way of Appearing by Mary Winfrey Trautmann. ISBN: 0-939416-04-2 8.95 paper.

Woman-Centered Pregnancy & Birth by the Federation of Feminist Women's Health Centers. ISBN: 0-939416-03-4 11.95 paper.

Fight Back! Feminist Resistance to Male Violence edited by Frédérique Delacoste & Felice Newman. ISBN: 0-939416-01-8 13.95 paper.

On Women Artists: Poems 1975-1980 by Alexandra Grilikhes. ISBN: 0-939416-00-x 4.95 paper.

Cleis Press is a nine year old women's publishing company committed to publishing progressive books by women. Order from the office nearest you: Cleis East, PO Box 8933, Pittsburgh PA 15221 or Cleis West, PO Box 14684, San Francisco CA 94114. Individual orders must be prepaid. Please add 15% shipping/handling. PA and CA residents add sales tax. MasterCard and Visa orders welcome—include account number, exp. date, and signature.